MOON LIGHT PRINCE

Karpov Kinrade

DARING
BOOKS

http://KarpovKinrade.com

Copyright © 2017 Karpov Kinrade
Cover Art Copyright © 2016 Karpov Kinrade
~~~~~
Published by Daring Books
~~~~~
First Edition
~~~~~
ISBN-10: 1939559480
ISBN-13: 9781939559487

For anyone who dreams of taking the Blood Oath.
The Princes of Hell are coming for you.
Are you ready?

TABLE OF CONTENTS

PROLOGUE

Kayla Windhelm

"The darkness takes shape. Small at first, then larger."
—Arianna Spero

I dream of fire and pain. I dream of Daison and Ari. And then, just as the flames threaten to consume me, he is there. Tavian Gray.

He holds me. And together we burn.

...

I wake gasping for breath, my head covered in sweat. I must have had a fever. Again. Too common now. Sickness. Ever since that bastard...ever since he...No. I cannot think about him. I cannot think about what happened. If I do, I will break. So I push away memories of Levi, memories of the dungeon, and I will myself to move. My limbs are weak, battered, cramped from days in a cell, but like a rusty door, eventually they give way.

My bones pop and crack as I sit up. My breath weighs heavy. And then, looking down, I see it. I see him.

I suppose I knew this day would come. I dreaded it. But now, seeing him on my lap, I can't help but smile. "Hello...Riku."

The little phoenix chirps back at me. He is a deep purple with streaks of silver, his feathers metallic in appearance. Slowly, I bring up my hand, move it forward like I do to calm horses.

Riku doesn't back away. Instead, he leans forward, into my palm, and I caress his feathers. They are soft, smooth, despite their solid looks. He seems to like my touch. He keeps rubbing against my arm, so I keep petting him, and he chirps in what sounds like happiness.

I can't help but giggle. Giggle. Me. A Shade who's just been through the worst days of her life, giggling on her bed with a tiny phoenix on her lap.

And he is tiny. About the size of a potato, easily fitting into my hand. Much smaller than I imagined.

"The mighty Riku," I say in mock seriousness, lifting him up to my face. "You are so cute."

He nods, beaming with his eyes. A mix of deep purple in the center and silver around the edges.

I had always thought Riku would be red, maybe orange. You know, fire colors. But my flame is inexplicably silver. So I suppose he matches me.

I force myself to sit up even more. Somehow, it hurts less now. Perhaps because of the cute baby phoenix in my hand. He hops onto my shoulder, perching there, and I glance at both of us in a polished steel oval that acts as a makeshift mirror. We look quite the pair, my blue hair complementing his deep purples. My pale skin matching his silver.

My gown is a simple green, unlike my very non-simple room. Fen insisted I stay in one of the bed chambers reserved for the most renowned guests within Stonehill. It's huge. Complete with a burning fireplace and a thick fur rug, bookshelves with more books than I've ever read, and even a vanity! Who needs all this stuff? Maybe a princess, but I'm no princess. I miss my own home, my small house outside the castle. And how Daison used to—

I push thoughts of him away, turning to Riku. "So hey, buddy, you hungry? You need any food?" I can't remember if Spirits need to eat. I try recalling if Ari ever feeds Yami, but can't remember. Then I think of Baron. Baron definitely eats food.

Still crazy to think he's a Spirit. When Fen told me all the details, my brain almost exploded. He'd been half Fae for centuries, but never knew the truth. How do these things happen?

I try not to ponder too heavily as I scour my room for food. Someone left an assorted meal of bread, cheese and ham on my dresser. I offer the ham to Riku, but he waves his little beak at me in a very displeased fashion. So I offer him the bread.

Then he chirps and digs in.

He's quite immaculate, getting every little crumb. "Good baby phoenix," I say, petting him on the head. "Now how about some water and—"

Footsteps. Outside my door.

My heart stops, my breath hitching. Please be Tavian. I ache to be with him. He's visited my room since we were freed, but I've been half asleep most of the time, battling fever. Today, I feel better than I have in ages. I need to see him.

I need—

The door opens.

It's not Tavian.

It's Asher.

"Ah, I see our new Druid has awoken." He closes the door, adjusting the black sleeves of his pristine suit. His dark hair is tidy, but messier than usual Asher. I wonder if something's happened.

"Can you see him?" I ask, raising my hand with Riku.

Asher nods. "Of course."

"And you're not surprised?"

"Why would I be?"

Because I haven't told anyone I'm a Druid. Not even Fen. Only Tavian. Only Tavian knows.

Asher seems to notice my pause. "I overheard your new friend talk about it. He seems quite nice."

So Tavian told him. Somehow, something feels wrong about the idea. I don't know Tavian well, but I know he's a private person. I don't imagine him spilling the secrets of others.

"I had my doubts," says Asher, waving his hands in the air. "But now that you have Riku, there's no denying it."

I drop my eyes, sighing. "No. I suppose there isn't."

"Come my dear," says Asher, putting a finger under my chin. "This is good news. We have three Druids on our side now. And the Midnight Star. Levi won't challenge us again."

I know he's trying to cheer me up, but at the mention of Levi I feel sick. I bend over, trying not to vomit, but preparing for it all the same.

Riku chirps soothingly in my ear, and it helps a bit.

"I know it can be...hard," continues Asher, "having responsibility thrust upon you. Even if you are raised to rule, the idea of ruling and the act of ruling are two very different things. As a Druid, you have a duty to your people. Maybe not as a supreme ruler, but as a guide. A mentor." He looks away, into the flames of the fireplace, his voice soft. "I feel much the same."

There is something about Asher today. A depth I have not seen before. Or perhaps, I am simply noticing a lack of wit. He seems more serious than usual.

"I don't believe the others know yet," says Asher. "That you're a Druid. If you wish, I could keep the secret a while longer."

"Yes," I say, suddenly feeling better and standing straighter. "That would be nice. Until I'm ready to tell them on my own."

"Very well. Now to important matters." He leans in, sniffing at my gown, then pulls back repulsed. "You must take a bath."

...

I only run into servants on my way to the bathhouse and none seem to notice Riku. He must be staying hidden, invisible. Dim light shines through the hallway windows. It must be very early. Explains the lack of people. When I enter the bath chamber, I am alone, in near darkness, the water a pale blue.

Well. I'm almost alone. There is Riku after all.

I slip off my gown and enter the water. It's warm, soothing to my aching joints. A slight steam hovers on its surface, the heat battling the cold air. I sigh and lean back against the bath walls, closing my eyes and letting my stress melt away.

"Hello, Princess."

I recognize his voice instantly. Deep and warm and gravelly.

Tavian Gray, tall, muscled and naked stands above me.

I think I...well...I think I forget how to think.

Then he smiles.

And my mind starts to wander. To things I could do to those muscles, those lips...

Then Tavian jumps in the pool, splashing me with water and breaking my wonderful dream.

I laugh and splash him back.

Before I can fully exact my revenge, he grabs my arms, pins them down, and presses his rock hard body against mine. His heart beats in time with my own. His breath tickles my skin. His scent is that of stone and wood and fire. I run a hand down his chest, studying every inch of his being, memorizing him as best I can. So I may never let go of this moment. So I can hold onto it forever.

"I missed you," I whisper, our lips close. Oh, so close...

"That is good." He places his mouth against my neck, kissing my skin gently over and over. "Otherwise, I would have stayed for nothing."

He recovered faster than me, somehow. I remember him by my bedside as I struggled to live. He seemed fine then. He seems fine now.

"What are you, Tavian Gray?" I ask, running my hand through his thick brown hair.

"You know who I am—"

KARPOV KINRADE

I yank on his hair. Just hard enough.

He inhales deeply, grinning. "I am many things. Right now, foremost, I am your friend."

"Just a friend?" I ask, biting my lip.

"Well, maybe I am a special friend."

I touch his face with my hands, tracing his sharp cheek bones, his sturdy chin.

Then he takes my face into his palms and pulls me closer. Closer. Closer.

Until our lips touch.

Until I feel his taste on my tongue.

It seems forever, until we part.

"Mmm," I say, still remembering him on my lips.

He chuckles. "Mmm is right." Then he puts a hand on my chin, his fingers rough and strong. He tilts my face until our eyes meet. "I will remember this, my princess. I will remember this for all time."

There is something to his words. A sadness.

And I realize what they mean.

"You're leaving, aren't you?"

He doesn't look away then. I think a lesser man would. But he does not. "Yes. This is not my world. Not my place. I am a traveler. And soon, I must travel again."

I grab his hand, holding it tightly, so tightly I fear I hurt him, but I don't care. "I can go with you."

"You are a Druid," he says glancing over my shoulder. And I realize he can see Riku standing there.

"Where you go, Fae will follow. They will seek your guidance, your leadership." He pauses, finally looking away, looking into the deep blue water. "I am no leader. I am no person to follow."

I shake my head, tears welling in my eyes. "Why? Why do you insist on being alone?"

"I…" He pauses. "Do you really wish to know?"

I nod, steeling myself for what is to come. "I do."

"Then stay with me tonight," he says, frowning. "The memories, they are worse than usual today. Stay with me, and you will see. Then you will understand."

I grip his hand even tighter. "I will stay with you. Show me."

...

We spend the day together, but it is not a happy affair. Not truly. Tavian seems lost, buried in his memories. While I eat ravenously, he barely touches his food. While I walk with a jump to my step, he lags behind. When I ask him what's wrong, "You will see," is all he says.

I try to find Fen, but Keeper Kal'Hallen informs me he and Dean are out searching for Ari. They should be back tomorrow.

I wish I could be out there, looking for my friend. But I am still too weak. Soon, though. I promise. Soon.

"She is very dear to you," Tavian remarks as we walk the gardens in fur cloaks.

"Yes," I say, thinking of Arianna. "She is like a sister. A sister I love."

He nods, not saying any more.

When night falls, he escorts me to a shack at the outskirts of the city—a place I thought abandoned. He seems to have made a home here. Thick rugs cover the floor and the fireplace is stocked with wood. He sets it burning, and we cuddle by the flames, warming each other.

I do not know how long we stay like this. Together. Holding each other.

But at some point, Tavian pulls away. "It is time I slept." He walks over to the corner, a cold, damp place. He grabs something there and tosses it at my feet. A sword.

"What is this?" I ask, not touching the blade.

"You may need it," he says.

"Why?"

He says nothing, laying down his fur robe and making a bed for himself.

"I've seen you sleep before," I say. "When we traveled."

"Not all nights are equal." He sounds tired, beaten. He lies down on the furs and closes his eyes. "Goodnight, Princess."

"Goodnight…"

He says no more.

Hours pass. Nothing. Nothing but a man sleeping peacefully. I fetch more wood for the fire. Keep it burning to stay warm.

It is sometime deep in the night, sometime when the moons are high, that Tavian begins to tremble. It starts with a murmur, a whisper I do not understand. He mumbles, louder, then louder, in a language I do not know. His hands start to shake at his words. His head jerks back and forth. He seems to be calling. Calling to someone. Yelling. Yelling a warning.

It is then the wind begins to stir. It howls around me though all windows are shut. It chills me despite the burning fire. The lights begin to dim. A shadow falls over the room.

I have seen this before. When Tavian threatened Metsi. When Tavian fought the raiders.

But now it happens as he sleeps.

He shakes and spasms, crying out. Screaming.

Thunder crashes.

But I see no lightning. No storm outside.

Thunder again. The tempest is here. In this room. The storm swirls around him.

A flash of light.

Another.

They blind me.

But in between the flashes, I catch glimpses.

Tavian.

Different.

His skin darker.

Darker.

Black.

White stripes upon his body.

His mouth twists unnaturally, opening, and he roars, tearing the air with his voice.

His teeth are far too long, far too sharp.

He is more beast than man now.

What is happening?

Riku screeches in terror, quivering on my shoulder.

Tavian roars again, and it is a sound of agony, such terrible agony.

I rush forward, wanting to shake him, to wake him, to make it stop.

But something stops me. A feeling. A feeling that this must pass on its own.

I hold back. Though every part of me wishes to help. I hold back.

Another flash.

And the fire goes out. Darkness envelops the room. Darkness and silence. A silence so strong it chills.

And then I hear it. Feel it.

His breath against my skin. The heavy breath of a beast.

He is in front of me.

I cannot see him. But I know he is there.

A predator before his prey.

I look for the sword, but can see nothing in the darkness. I search with my hands, but find nothing.

The breath is still upon me. Hot. Loud.

Something growls in the darkness.

My fingers find purchase. The sword. I hold it up.

Don't make me do this. Don't make me do this.

Something lunges. Lunges for my throat.

I drive the sword forward.

And as quickly as the darkness came, it withdraws.

The flames return, flickering.

And before me, I see Tavian covered in sweat, shaking on the floor, bleeding from his shoulder.

"No," I fall to my knees, pulling him to me, holding me tight. "I'm sorry. I'm so sorry."

He lets his head fall back, fall back so we are eye to eye. And I see it is him again, the real him. "I told you, Princess," he says, his voice a raspy whisper. "I told you I must go."

My hands shake. My eyes fill with tears. I tear away a piece of my gown and wrap it around his bleeding shoulder. The wound is not deep, thank the Spirits. "What happened?" I ask as I work, my voice trembling.

"You remember what I told you? How I summoned the Darkness? How I watched it kill my family? There is something else." He clenches his jaw, every word a clear effort. "The Darkness spared those who performed the ritual from death. But it did not spare us entirely. A curse it placed upon us. A curse…"

He reaches for something. The table. Water. He must want water. I rush, grabbing a cup and putting it to his lips. He drinks.

I caress his hair softly, waiting. When he is done, I take back the cup. "What is your curse?" I ask.

"I cannot forget," he says. "I cannot forget anything. The Darkness consuming my wife. The screams of my children as they died. I remember all of it. Every single detail. Every single detail I have ever felt."

"What do you mean?" I ask, frowning, feeling his pain.

He clears his throat, raising his voice. "Do you remember the last time you touched hot iron? The last time you burned your hand? Do you remember how it truly felt? The pain?"

"No," I say, realizing what he means. I can recall a part of the pain, but only a part.

"I remember everything," he says. "Every cut. Every burn."

"That is…That is…"

"Horrible?" He smiles for a moment. "Imagine if women could remember childbirth. If they could remember every detail. Had to live with it every day."

"It would drive one mad," I say, sipping some of the water myself.

"It would, wouldn't it?" He pauses. "Most times, I can distract myself with the present. But the past is always there, always by my side, haunting me. Mocking me with every mistake. Every tragedy. For a time, I can ignore its call. But some days it is harder not to listen. And then...then I live in agony."

"I'm so sorry," I say, tears running down my cheek. "I'm so sorry."

He raises an eyebrow, seemingly puzzled. "It is not your fault, Princess. It is my own burden. A burden well deserved."

"No one deserves such a fate."

He shakes his head. "If you could know how my family suffered, if you could know as I know, you would not agree." He tries to push me away.

I don't let him. I hold him tighter. "But you didn't intend to harm them."

"No. No, I didn't. But I must still pay for what I did. For the fool I was."

He pushes me away then, stronger than I expected. I fall back, wiping my tears, Riku chirping into my ear as Tavian grabs his belongings. He wraps his cloak around his shoulders and heads to open the door.

He pauses, holding the handle. "I will leave tomorrow. It is best. Best for me to travel alone. And...I will not tell anyone about Riku. About what you truly are. That is your burden to bear."

With that he opens the door and leaves.

A sharp cold wind hits me, and I wrap myself in the fur rug. Tavian's rug. It smells of him. And I hold it close. Weeping. Weeping for what could have been.

It is hours later, near day, when I remember what Tavian said. What he truly said. *I will not tell anyone about Riku. About what you truly are. That is your burden to bear.*

Your burden. Your burden. Your burden…

If Tavian kept my secret, then how did Asher know? How did he know?

I grab my fur cloak and run out into the cold winter air. I run back to the castle. There, in an empty hallway, I find Asher. Despite the hour, he is awake, and he walks with a purpose.

I stay in the shadow, trailing him through winding pathways and doors.

Once, I close a door too loudly, and Asher glances back. I freeze, slipping away into a corner. Asher looks around, then shrugs and continues on.

I follow more carefully. Riku, fortunately, doesn't make a sound.

He knows something is wrong here. Something we must uncover.

Asher stops in the middle of a hall, peeks around over his shoulder, then pushes something on the wall. A stone.

A groan echoes through floor, and a piece of the wall slides away. A secret door?

I thought I knew the passages. Fen showed me all of them.

But this. This is not one I know of.

Asher enters the new door, disappearing from sight.

What is he doing? Meeting someone?

Oh, Asher, please don't be a traitor. Please.

I clench my jaw and follow, hoping for the best, dreading the worst. I follow through the secret door, down steps leading deep into the earth. Leading to a chamber shrouded in darkness, lit only a by a few torches casting sinister shadows. Behind a corner, I watch as Asher grabs something from the floor. A tray of food.

He carries it forward. To something in the center of the room.

No. Not something. Someone. A man, bloody and bruised. On his knees. His hand outstretched, bound in chains.

I whisper an incantation, enhancing my night vision. And then I see the prisoner's face.

This...this doesn't make any sense.

The prisoner...the prisoner is Asher?

The man, the prisoner, looks up, and he grins. "No one figure you out yet? Bloody marvelous. Means I still get to be the one who kills you."

It sure sounds like Asher. The voice. The inflections. Even the cocky wit.

The other Asher, the one standing, laughs. It is not his voice. No. It's deeper now. Darker. Familiar.

My gut twists. My hands tremble. It can't be...

The other Asher waves his hand, and his form shimmers, changes. And there he stands.

My father.

Lucian.

Despite myself, memories flash through my mind. Memories of my mother escorting me to High Castle. My first trip there. Waiting for hours in the hall. Hours to see the king. Getting our chance. Walking up to the great king in front of hundreds of people. Oh, how mighty he looked. How grand. Dark hair with only streaks of gray. Black armor covering his body like dragon scales. A mighty sword by his throne, surely too big for any normal man. My mother pushed me forward to stand before him. "This is your daughter," she said.

The king looked at me then. Once. Only once he looked.

"My only daughter is dead," he said.

But, what did he mean? I could not understand. I was his daughter, and I was surely not dead. He was my father. Father's take care of their children. They embrace them. Tell them words of wisdom.

But the king did not move to touch me. He did not speak to share with me a story. Instead, he waved his hand in a gesture, and my mother pushed me to move out of the way. I did not wish to move. I wished to stay. To talk with father. But my mother pushed me more. "Please," she whispered. "Before the guards notice."

I let her move me then, move me back into the crowd. I had seen the guards. Big men in scary helmets that looked like beasts. I did not want those men to notice me. So I went back to the crowd, and then I went home. I did not see my father again. Not for a long time.

But I see him now.

He stands before me.

Laughing.

Laughing at the real Asher.

He's been impersonating him. Using illusion for... who knows how long.

I once thought Lucian dead. Gone. But he lives. He keeps my half-brother prisoner. I don't know what game he plays, but I know it is not good. Lucian was... is...never good.

"What's so funny?" asks Asher. The real Asher.

Lucian stops chuckling, adjusting his red cape. "Your audacity, my son. You always were so full of yourself, so proud."

"Ha, ha, ha," Asher says in mock laughter. "The Prince of Pride is prideful. Oh father, you truly are hilarious. Please tell me, what was your curse again? Bad jokes?"

Something changes then.

Lucian grows still. Cold. This is the man I know. The man I saw that day in court.

"I wish we could chat more, my son," says the king, his voice plain, bereft of emotion, "but we are being rude. You see, we have a guest."

A guest?

I freeze.

He means me.

Lucian turns, facing me. And he smiles. "Oh, Kayla, Kayla, right on time."

What does he mean?

"Come now," says Lucian. "Come out of the shadows."

I do as he says, not because he says it. But because this way I can raise my sword. Raise my sword and point it straight at his heart. "Let him go."

"Not yet. The time is not right. But soon. I promise."

"No!" I yell, stepping forward. I don't know my plan. I don't have one. I can't fight Lucian. But maybe, with Riku at my side, maybe I stand a chance...

"You won't need that thing," says the king, gesturing at my blade. "Don't you see, you are here for a reason. No one. No one has uncovered the truth. No one knows I have been impersonating a prince. No one but you. A filthy half-breed wench. Why is that?"

"Because you let me," I say, realizing the truth. "You lied about Tavian on purpose. You led me here."

"Hmm," says Lucian, nodding. "Perhaps you are smarter than I thought. Smarter than your whore mother, anyway."

"Don't talk about her," I hiss. "Don't you dare!"

He shrugs. That's all? A shrug?

"How did you know I was a Druid?" I ask, studying the room. Looking for other exits. Looking for a way to free Asher.

"It is a skill I have learned," says Lucian, "to sense power in others. Your Spirit is strong. Ever since we rescued you from the dungeon, I knew what you were. Your potential."

"Do you? Really?" I raise my free hand, and it lights with silver flame. "Then you know what I can do to you. Let Asher go. Now. Or I burn you until there is nothing but ash."

Asher's eyes go wide. "Kayla. Kayla you can't—"

Lucian slaps him across the face. "Quiet. Let the half-breed play her games. It will be all the better when she loses."

Asher drops his head. He seems barely conscious.

I'm tired of this talk. Of Lucian's insults. I've carried a lifetime of hate for this man. And now I unleash it.

I charge forward, and Riku launches into the air. His wings burn bright with flame. Like an arrow, he flies for Lucian.

But the king is too quick. He steps to the side, avoiding the flames, and he dashes forward. At me.

Our blades clash.

And in an instant, it is over.

My sword falls to the floor.

He disarmed me. I do not even know how. He moves so fast. It's impossible.

He—

Lucian kicks me in the gut, and I fall, clutching my stomach. I spit and blood flies from my mouth, staining the cold stones.

Riku screeches in fury and strikes, claws reaching for Lucian's face.

The king grabs the phoenix midair. Holds him by the neck.

"No," I try to yell, but it comes out a weak whimper.

Riku chirps in terror, thrashing, but Lucian does not let go. He seems unaffected by the burning feathers. Maybe his armor protects him. Maybe he truly feels no pain.

"Silver flame," he says, his eyes wide with awe. "There hasn't been a silver flame for ages. Not according to the ancient Fae texts. You truly are special." He looks at Riku with pleasure. With greed.

"Let him go!" With the last of my strength, I jump up, grab my sword and strike at his arm.

Lucian blocks with one hand. It's all he needs. He smacks the blunt of his blade against my fingers, crushing them, and I drop my blade again. Any energy I had leaves me, and I fall to my knees, crying, pleading. "Please let him go. Let him go."

I cannot stand the pain Riku is in. The terror. It is my pain. My terror.

Lucian pulls something from his red cloak. A grey stone. He holds it up and whispers something under his breath. Words I do not understand. Words like Tavian mumbled in his sleep.

Riku screeches again. Louder. A sound of true horror.

Something. Something is happening.

Riku becomes more flame than bird. His screams fade. They die out.

And then nothing is left. Nothing but silver smoke.

It flows into the grey stone, changes it. Turns it a deep purple with streaks of silver.

"What have you done to him?" I scream, my body shaking with terror and rage.

"Shhh," says Lucian, caressing the stone. "Do not worry, my dear. Riku is safe. Safe and well."

He's in the stone. The bastard put Riku in the stone. "What do you want with him?"

"I need his help. And then he will be free. I swear." He smiles at me.

I spit at his face.

The phlegm doesn't reach him. But I don't care.

Lucian just shakes his head. A strange disappointment in his eyes.

"What now?" I ask. "Chain me up just like you did your son?"

He raises an eyebrow, then sits down to my level. "Oh no, there's no reason for that. No, I have a far simpler solution." He pulls something from his cloak. A vial. A potion.

No. Not again. I'm not taking something again.

"Don't be afraid, my dear. This will simply make you sleep. A deep, beautiful sleep. Your friends will think the fever broke you, that Levi's tortures and poisons put you into a coma in the end. They will try to help you, but nothing will work."

I lean back. "No. Please."

He doesn't look into my eyes. He doesn't seem to hear. "But you will wake. One day. When the time is right. When I have need of you."

"No. Please—"

He grabs my jaw. I try to keep it closed, but he pries it open. Stuffs the vial down my throat. The liquid pours down, coating my tongue with bitterness. I try not to swallow, but it's gagging me. Gagging me until my muscles react against my will. My mind begins to fade. My vision blurs. His is the last face I see. The face of my father.

"Good," he whispers. "Good."

1

BLEED FOR ME

"Sometimes wolves come in sheep's clothing."
—Fenris Vane

They won't kill me. *At least not yet.* As far as words of consolation go, these are pretty pathetic, but they're all I have. They're the words I whisper to myself when Metsi comes in each morning to administer my dose of prenatal herbs by having her lackey force my jaw open as she pours the bitter liquid down my throat. They're the words I use to quiet my mind at night when I am left alone save for the sound of the wind and wild animals outside my barred window. They're the words I think to myself each morning when I lurch out of bed to vomit up my morning sickness into a pail they left for me. I don't know if this is caused by my pregnancy, or by the herbs Metsi gives me—but each day I feel worse.

It only took a week for these words to replace *dum spiro spero* in my mind. I still have hope, deep down, buried where my magic now lays dormant. I have tried to cast spells, but my magic is a dead thing inside me, there but useless. They've placed wards on my room to ensure I cannot use magic, and it works.

It's not a fancy room, but it's not a dungeon. So there's that. I have a small mattress on the floor that's clean and warm. A room in which to bathe and relieve myself. And three changes of clothes so that I don't stink. And there's one window, always left open, but barred with lead to keep me from escaping. My door is always locked. There are no decorations. Nothing to occupy my mind save the occasional book Metsi brings in to let me read—mostly very dry books about the history of the Fae.

Each day I get a walk to keep the baby healthy. The walk involves following Metsi and her guard down to the dungeons, where I endure an hour of watching them torture Levi.

As I sit and watch right now, my stomach clenches and bile rises in my throat. It is suffocatingly hot down here, with no ventilation and fires burning that smell of flesh. The air is acrid and stale and reeks of blood, sweat and excrement. I cannot control my vomiting when I'm down here, so Metsi hands me a bucket, but refuses to allow me to go back to my room.

"I would think you would enjoy watching this monster suffer," Metsi says, holding up a knife, the tip red hot from the fire she held it in. "After all, did you not suffer at his hands? Did you not see the effects of what he did to your friend Kayla? To the people you claim to love? He is getting nothing less than what he deserves."

Her next words are drowned out by the screaming. Levi no longer looks like a man, but rather like a charred, skinned wild thing that just wants to be put out of its misery.

And Metsi's not entirely wrong. There was a time I would have paid to see Levi get his comeuppance. A time I would have volunteered to exact justice from his flesh. A pound for a pound. But I didn't know what I know now. I didn't know that seeing someone tortured, seeing someone suffer beyond measure, takes its toll on your soul, no matter what that person did to deserve it. I didn't know how vile it would feel to watch what I am now forced to watch.

Today, after Metsi is done with Levi, she turns to me with a cruel smile. "I have something to take care of, but since you are under contract to spend time with each of the princes, I'll leave you two alone to bond. Consider it quality time with this month's monster."

We are not left alone of course. Two armed guards are stationed on the other side of the door. But we are

3

alone enough. More alone than we've been in a long time.

One of his eyes is swollen shut by an ugly bruise. His other eye is bloodshot. There are pieces of skin missing from his body, and burns that are festering. On the table next to him sits a variety of torture devices, as well as a cup of human blood, to help him heal in small increments, just enough to wound him again.

I don't think they've let him sleep since we've arrived, though he has likely passed out for short periods.

I have no idea what to say to him. I hate him. Loathe him. When I think of the things he's done to me, to my friends, to my people, I feel a ball of rage twisting in my gut, fighting for space with the inexplicable life that now grows inside of me. But seeing him suffer makes me want to help. To heal. To fix. Of course, I can't do that either. There's nothing I can do to ease his suffering, even if I wished to. So I sit. And wait.

"You're next," he says through a mouthful of blood.

"What?"

"You're next. What they're doing to me, they'll do to you."

I shake my head. "They need me too much," I remind him. "They don't need you."

His lips curl up in a grotesque smile that's filled with cruelty even still. "They need what's in your womb, not you."

4

"Pregnancies take time," I say. "I'll find a way out of this by then."

The first thing I did when I had a moment alone, right after my capture, was summon Fen with my blood and his demon mark. But if the magic worked—which is doubtful given the wards—he has not come. Or maybe can't come. I have no idea what became of him and the others once I was captured. I can only hope and pray they are safe. And Es and Pete, my god, I brought them into this messed up world and left them stranded here. And there's nothing I can do about any of it until I find a way to escape.

I place a hand on my stomach, something I've been doing a lot of lately. It's hard to think about this baby. To think that it belongs to me and Fen. In my world, I wouldn't even know I'm pregnant yet, but magic has perks, and one of them is apparently early pregnancy detection.

"You think I deserve this, don't you?" says Levi, his head hanging low, but eyes fixed on me. "You think this is justice?"

I don't say anything. I won't give him my pity.

"There was a time, you know," continues Levi, "a time when I was no danger to anyone. I was but a boy, bright and eager to learn. But the world took that boy and forged him into a harsh man. It didn't have to be that way, but it was." He pauses, glaring into the fireplace burning within the stones.

"I still remember, back in the Silver Gardens, back when mother and father still lived. I remember being lost. Younger than Niam and Zeb, but older than Dean, Ace and Asher. Somehow, my older brothers were praised for being wise and mature, my younger ones for being spirited and youthful, and yet I was not praised at all. I didn't let it deter me though, no, not at first. I took hard to my studies, exceling in my classes and impressing my tutors. I grew found of smithing especially, and toiled long hours to perfect the craft. When testing came, I worked for weeks on a blade, pouring my ambitions and dreams into the steel. Gold it was, with a sapphire in the guard. Lightbringer, I called it. And when it was finally done, I took it to my father, eager to impress him for once. He glanced at the blade and laughed. 'Oh Levi, you couldn't possibly make such a blade,' he said. 'Tell me, who'd you steal it from?' I argued with him. Told him it truly was my work. But he just laughed once more and left for more important matters. I took the blade back to the forge then and bashed it until it shattered. I didn't forge again."

He turns his face back to me. "When the next testing came, I did as my father expected. I stole the project, a handmade cloak, from Ace and passed it off as my own. My father congratulated me more than he did before." He chuckles, then his eyes grow darker. "Ace and I fought after that, but not for long. He forgave me, though he had no reason. He just…did."

He pauses much longer this time.

I cross my arms. "So what? I'm supposed to forgive you? Is that the point of this story? Poor Levi had one bad thing happen to him, and instead of working harder to prove others wrong, he just did what they expected and turned bad? Well, boo hoo. We all have crap to deal with. At least you have brothers who care for you—"

"You think they care for me?" He flips back his head and laughs. "Really? You think Niam sides with me because he cares about poor old Levi? No, Princess. He sides with me because of the opportunities he sees for his own gain. The schemes he plots to undercut me. And who else do you think *cares* for me? Zeb, perhaps? Oh, no, Zeb does as he pleases, dear Princess. Sometimes he helps, and other times he stabs in the back. For centuries, he's darted back and forth between me and Asher, and he will flip sides once again. In fact...I'm not sure who he supports even now. Do you know, Princess? Are you sure?"

I stay silent, because he's not wrong. I don't know who Zeb supports. I don't even know if he voted for Fen and me to die, or if he tried to save us.

Levi grins at my silence, then continues. "And I hope you have no illusions about Asher and Fen. They despise me, I can assure you."

"Only because you've made it so," I say. "Only because you betray and hurt them every chance possible."

"Like when?" He looks up, as if he's trying to remember something. "Like when I witnessed the Presenting? The one Dean and Asher joined in as well? I understand it was hard for you, Princess, but you must understand such things are not rare in Inferna. Slaves are presented all the time, even free men sometimes, if they are looking for particular work. You may find the custom disgusting, but my brothers do not, I assure you. Well, perhaps save Fen. He is an odd one.

"Now, let me see, what else? Oh, perhaps I betrayed them when we went to battle with the Fae? No, wait. I don't believe that's right. I believe I fought at their side, while you hid the fact that you were the Midnight Star, the fact that you had returned the Druids from their slumber.

"Or perhaps you refer to the time when I threatened you. When I saw what you truly were, and I tried to end your life. When I tried to stop the war and save the lives of all in Inferna. Even the lives of innocent Fae.

"Or perhaps you refer to the time when I—along with five other Princes of Hell—sentenced you and Fen to death, the Midnight Star who brought ruin upon my people and the Earth Druid who had slain our father."

He pulls on his chains in rage. "I may have threatened you, Princess, hurt you even. But I have never betrayed my brothers."

I...I don't know what to say. He has hurt me, nearly killed me, and I always assumed he had done worse to others...but I have never seen him do harm to his brothers. Never even seen him act alone. I forget that Dean and Asher were part of the Presenting, even peripherally. I forget they were part of the Council who voted for my death.

This is a cruel world. I have let myself forget, but no longer. Before I came here, I had never killed anyone, never been taken captive or seen others tortured. Now I have endured all these things. And I know I will endure more.

Levi has done terrible things, but what of me?

I have killed.

I have lied.

I have ruined.

My very existence causes chaos and disorder. My very presence brings death and pain.

"There is a way to escape, you know," Levi whispers. "Quite simple, really."

"What? What do you mean?"

He adjusts his neck, twisting it to the side until the bones pop. "You let me feed on your blood. I will regain my strength. Then I can break these shackles with ease."

"And kill me," I say, backing away.

He smiles. "Kill you? True. I would. But you are not just you now, are you? I've heard of the babe you carry. My niece or nephew. The heir. What kind of uncle would I be if I killed the child? What kind of monster would I be?"

I shake my head, placing a protective hand on my belly. "You really expect me to believe that? That you care about my and Fen's baby?"

"Believe what you will." He shrugs. "The way I see it, I am your only option. Let me feed, and together we can escape. Don't, and you will remain a prisoner forever. That is, until your baby is born. And then what do you think will happen, Princess? Let me tell you. Metsi will cut your throat and take the babe as her own. She will teach the child to call *her* mother. And your precious babe will grow up just like her mommy Druid, demented, mad, a Fae who will not stop until every vampire and Shade is massacred. Is that want you want for your child? Is that the future you imagine?"

"Screw you," I say through gritted teeth. I'm not stupid. Of course I've considered that. But I will figure something out before that happens. I must.

He chuckles.

A part of his offer tempts me, but I would be a fool to take it. Even if he's not lying about protecting the baby, he has no reason to take me with him. He could flee on his own.

"There is one other way," says Levi. "You could…" He glances at the guards at the door and lowers his voice further. So quiet.

"What? How?" I lean closer to listen.

And then he grabs me.

His hand clutches my hair and yanks my head to his mouth. Before I can react, his lips brush my neck. His teeth sink into my skin.

I gasp as blood rushes out of me. I try to fight. Kick and scream. But already, he has grown stronger. He keeps a hold of me. Drinking. Drinking.

Yelling.

The guards.

They charge at Levi.

For a moment, he lets me go.

With bare hands, he tears the guards apart, their entrails exploding onto the walls. I fall to the ground. Weak. So weak. I try to stand. To crawl. I cannot.

And then Levi returns. To finish.

He grabs me by the neck. Bites down again.

I can't even scream this time.

He is draining me. Draining me completely.

I am fading. I am dying.

He never cared for the baby. He was lying all along. Of course, he would just kill me. With me gone, the Druids would have to return to slumber. Metsi's powers would fade. The war would be over. And Levi could escape with ease.

He is close now. Close to ending it all.

My vision blurs. My mind dims.

I place my hands on my belly. On my baby. And I think of Fen.

I'm so sorry. I'm so sorry to you both. You deserved a life together.

Someone rushes into the room. Water crashes into Levi, pushing him back.

But it is too late.

I am too far gone.

I close my eyes.

And I die.

2

SILENCE

Fenris Vane

*"Our father, King Lucian. He could be...dif-
ficult, at times, but he was always fair."*
—Asher

I feel it. The bond breaking. Something is wrong.

Arianna!

I rush forward through snow and brush, searching, hoping, praying. Branches snap beneath my feet
and dust flies in my wake. Baron keeps pace beside me,
running faster then he ever has, never slowing, even
when his breath draws ragged and fatigue settles into
his bones. For a straight day, we run. We run. We run.
Until we can run no more. As the sun begins to set, I fall
to my knees on a hill overlooking the forest. My breath
is heavy. My body is drenched with sweat beneath layers of brown fur cloaks and vests. Baron moans into the

snow, his body as spent as mine, his howls weak and plaintive. We have searched for days. Weeks. But still we find nothing. And now…now something has changed.

Ever since I fed on Arianna that day in the cave, I have felt bonded to her, felt her life a part of my own. But now I feel it no longer. Instead, I am empty. Hollow. Alone.

It is time for a new plan. Time to reassess. Time to do something I do not wish to do, but I must. For Arianna. Because I know of no other path now. I draw my dagger and slice the palm of my hand. With red blood, I draw *his* mark.

Then I set to building a fire behind a group of large stones. They remind me of a claw, viscous and cruel, reaching for the heavens. *You are the Prince of War*, they seem to whisper. *You are the Prince of Death. What ending did you dream of? Did you dream of happiness?*

My body coils with rage at my own dark thoughts. It burns with a fury I have not felt in my long life, even at my darkest. And then I fling my head back and roar to the stars. I smash my fist into the ground and feel it shake beneath me. Again. Again. I strike the ground until my knuckles bleed, and then I strike again.

And when I have no strength left, I fall back, back against those cold cruel stones, and I lose myself in memories. Memories of Arianna in my arms, her soft skin upon my own, her lips against mine. Her breath a cool breeze upon my ear, her scent like fresh flowers and a summer day. Oh, how I long to have her back in my arms. To know I can keep her safe, to whisper words of comfort. Why did I ever let her go? Why did I not see her rush for Levi? Why, when I did, could I not fight through the guards fast enough? Why? Why? Why? The word haunts me.

But I will not fall into despair. Not yet.

I will save Arianna. I will do anything to do so.

I would even summon *him*.

Baron stands at attention, sniffing at the air.

He comes from the shadows, a silent snake coming upon its prey. I look up. Glare into his dark eyes.

"Lucian."

My father smiles, but there is no warmth to his eyes. He is cold and harsh like the storm. Black and red armor clads his body. His great sword hangs on his back. "You wish to speak," he says, still half in the shadows, half hidden in darkness. As if the light from my fire would burn him.

I have not seen my father since the day I drugged him. The day I thought him dead and my entire world changed. I stand, equaling him in height, my body as massive as his own. I never look away. Never show a sign of weakness. "Where is she?"

He does not feign ignorance. Feigning ignorance is feigning dullness. "The Druid Metsi has her. In a place you will never find. A place she will never escape."

It is as I feared. I saw the broken ice. The raging water. The Water Druid has her. I clench my jaw. "Without Arianna, the contract cannot be honored. A new King of Hell cannot be chosen. You must help bring her back."

He chuckles. "I must? After you betrayed me, your own father, your own kin?"

"I was never yours," I roar.

"Of course you were mine. I raised you. My wife's blood brought you to life, flows through your veins even now." His words pulse with rage. He is more upset than I imagined. Upset at the thought I am not his own. Or perhaps just upset I am not within his power.

"If the contract is not honored," I continue, "the realms will suffer. There will be no ruler, and your children will continue to squabble as they have, setting ruin upon each other. Have you seen the destruction within my castle? Have you seen the strung-up Fae and the dismembered heads adorning pikes?" I step forward, pleading. "Did you not seek to bring balance between the Fae and vampire? Did you not seek to bring peace? Help me. Help me save Arianna and bring balance."

He looks down for the first time. "Even if I could… even if I did…what would it matter? You have no desire to be king. You will make no difference."

His words punch me in the gut. They ring true, and yet, they fill me with anger. How dare he deign to know my mind? To know what I can or cannot do?

"I will bring peace," I vow. "I will bring balance."

Lucian smirks, pointing at me. "You have always had a flair for the grand gestures, a flair for the dramatic. And often, you have kept to your word, succeeded where others thought you'd fail. But this time, you will not succeed my son. You cannot. Because this time, you are against me." He looks to the fire. "You and your brothers play your game, fighting over my scraps like a pack of dogs, but in the end, there is only one King of Hell. And he stands before you." He turns to leave.

But I will not let him. My voice thunders through the air. Asking what I have dreaded to ask. "Am I a true Prince of Hell? Can Arianna choose me to rule?"

He turns back, his face half in shadow, half in light. "Yes. She may choose you. But will you let her?"

His words fill me with emotion. I am a true heir. Arianna and I can still be together. But before I can collect all my thoughts, Lucian continues.

"You know, I despised you at first," he says. "Despised everything you represented. A Fae living in my own home, feeding upon my food, my hospitality, my knowledge. But in time, you showed me something I never thought true. You showed me it is not our birth that makes us who we are, it is our choices. It is our own true self." His eyes fill with sorrow; an emotion I do not recall ever seeing on him. "I once thought myself condemned to this realm, condemned to live a life lesser than that of my brother's. But you showed me I could do anything. Anything. I remember when you left to slay the beast upon Grey Mountain. It was your test, your test to see if you were worthy of a realm of your own. Half your brothers laughed and placed bets on your demise, the other half worried and trembled for your safety. But I...I did not doubt you then. Too often had you proven me wrong. Too often had you made dreams reality. So when you returned from Grey Mountain, your rags soaked in blood, the head of the beast strapped to your belt, I did not even blink an eye. That is Fenris, I said. That is who he is. The Prince of War."

Why does he tell me all this? "You care nothing for me," I hiss.

"Oh, I care, my son. I care for you all. It is why I do what I do. One day, you will understand. It is why I tell you this now. So you remember. Remember I am always on your side."

His words sound of lies, but I will use them as I can. "If you are on my side, then help me. Tell me where Arianna is. If you do not, I swear I will never forgive you. I will hunt you. I will do as others think I've done, and you will fall upon my blade."

Inexplicably, he smiles. "Perhaps one day, my son. Perhaps one day." And as fast as he came, he slips away into the shadows.

I run forward, grasping for him. But he is already gone. Vanished by the magic he shares with no one.

And I am once again alone.

I fall back against those stones, and I draw another mark.

It is morning by the time Dean finds me. He wears no shirt despite the cold, only black pants, a sword on his hip, a bow strung across his shoulder. His golden hair shimmers in the sun. He grimaces when he sees me. "No luck?"

"Some." I say, putting out the fire. "She is with the Druid Metsi, but where I do not know."

"And you came upon this knowledge how, exactly?"

"Our father."

Dean's eyes almost leave his skull. "He came to you?"

"Yes. He answered my summons." I throw my supplies back over my shoulder and head for the next mountain.

Dean follows, his legs sinking up to his knees in the snow. He has searched these lands as I have these past few days. He has scouted day and night but found nothing. "So what next? We continue to scour the Outlands?"

"No," I say, sighing, wishing I did not have to share this knowledge. But Dean is the only prince to lend me his aid. Even Asher refuses to search. The Prince of Pride hasn't been himself lately, but I have neither the time nor attention to find out what ails my brother. "There is another place," I tell Dean. "Another place where the Fae dwell." And then I tell him about Avakiri.

"I heard whispers. Rumors of rumors." Dean shakes his head in wonder. "But I thought them false tales conjured to give the Fae hope. If this place does indeed exist, can you imagine the history we will find there? The culture?"

I shrug. "I only hope we find Arianna."

Dean grins like a child promised candy. "So do you know how we get to this…Avakiri?"

"Varis and I spoke of it briefly. Before he left to search the skies for Arianna." The Druid has not sent word for weeks. I hope he is safe. He likely returned to Avakiri, hoping to find the Midnight Star, and if what he said was true, his people would not have welcomed him with open arms.

"There is a door nearby," I continue. "A Waystone, they call it. A passage into Avakiri. I do not know if I will be able to open it, but I will try. My Druid blood may be enough. Should be enough."

Dean nods, and then we do not speak for a while as I guide him over freezing mountains and through dense forests. Baron stays close to my heel as we walk, and I occasionally lay a hand on his head as my thoughts turn to the days after Arianna disappeared.

Dean, Asher, and I met to discuss plans. Small parties had been sent out to search for Arianna already, but they returned with no news, and we could scarce afford the extra manpower when every body was needed here.

Es and Pete, her best friends, had volunteered to search as well, but they did not know the land nor how to defend themselves in the wild. So Dean escorted them back to earth, after a long talk that involved alcohol and promises to keep them informed the moment we found Arianna. So we had to reassess, and I needed advice.

The Prince of Pride adjusted his collar, cursing under his breath, then turned to the map before us. "How will you find her?" he asked. "Where will you start?"

I pointed at the different Outland villages and forts scattered across the map. "Dean and I will travel north, leaving no stone unturned, sweeping across the entire border. We will—"

"You won't find her," said Asher. "You didn't find her before. And you won't find her now."

Dean tilts his head to the side. "It was you who brought her back the first time the Fae took her, wasn't it, Asher? Perhaps you can offer some advice instead of whining."

"Very well," said Asher, sitting down and adjusting his black suit. "Send the Druid after her. He knows the Fae better than us all. If they have her, and they likely do, he will know where to look."

Dean nodded, twirling a finger through his blond curls. "Sounds pretty good, actually. But what if she's not with the Fae? What if Levi has her?"

I shook my head. "There have been no reports of him. Likely, he is dead or taken as well."

Dean frowned, searching the map. "Or perhaps he took Arianna somewhere secret. Perhaps he is trying to...guarantee his ascension."

If he were to get her pregnant and turn her into a vampire, then the contract would be fulfilled. Her time with the other princes would be forfeited, and Levi would become king of all. The thought disgusted me. The thought of Levi and Arianna somewhere alone. The thought of him...

I could not even imagine it.

"If that were true," I said, "and Levi did indeed have her in his clutches, I think he would have returned triumphant by now. Instead, it has been days."

"It has," agreed Asher. "So why not do as I propose and send the Druid? He will fair far better than the two of you."

I clenched my jaw. It was true that Dean and I had already begun to search and found nothing. But we had not strayed too far from the castle yet. My castle. "We must look farther north," I said. "We will leave today."

"And who will run Stonehill?" asked Asher. "Who will watch the Moonlight Garden?"

"I suppose it has to be you," I said. "Don't worry. It won't be all that difficult. The Keepers will tell you what needs attention."

Asher mock-laughed. "Not that difficult? Running three realms? You must be out of your mind."

Dean shrugged, pouring himself a glass of wine. "I find it pretty easy."

"That is because your realm is built on alcohol and sex," said Asher. "But other realms are not so simple."

Dean snickered. "Yeah, some are built on nail polish and flowers. *So* difficult."

Asher jumped from his chair and pinned Dean against the wall. He gripped him by the collar and pushed him up to the air. "You will not insult me again. Do you understand?"

There was a panic in Dean's eyes. And then it turned to laughter. "Smooth Asher losing his temper. Times are changing, indeed. What next, brother? Shall we jump into an arena and spar? I so look forward to kicking your ass."

Asher's eye twitched, and he seemed about ready to fight, but instead he sighed and let his brother go. "I have more important things to do than fight you, Dean." And then Asher left the room, avoiding both our gazes.

I kept my eyes on him as he disappeared down the hall. "He is acting strange," I said.

Dean nodded. "So you've noticed it, too."

"So have I." A third voice. A new voice. The Druid. Varis stepped in from the balcony, his white clock drifting in a wind I could not feel. His bald head gleaming in the torch light as his silver white owl perched on his shoulder. He must have flown there silently. How long had he been listening?

"Asher and I have spoken briefly," continued the Druid. "He was…nicer than usual."

I raised an eyebrow. "Nicer? And this is an odd thing between you? Considering you two were—"

"Yes. It is odd," said Varis, cutting me off. "After what we have been through, our talks are full of sorrow and regrets. At least, they used to be. Now he is too polite. Too formal."

Dean rubbed his chin. "Polite? You're right. Something is wrong with Asher."

"We should keep an eye on him," I say. A thought tickles at my mind. What if…no. It couldn't be illusion. He is too identical to the brother I know. It would take great knowledge and great power to cast such a spell. No one would be capable of it. No one I have ever heard of.

I turned to the Druid. "Varis, tonight we leave to search for Arianna."

He bowed his head. "Then I shall leave as well. Zyra and I will search the skies."

Dean looked hesitant. "So we leave Asher alone to rule our realms?"

"Only for a while," I said. "Besides, what harm can he do? The realms are ancient. They are hard to change from their ways. And if he does something disagreeable, then we will undo it upon our return." I pause. "Though these circumstances are not ideal, Arianna must come first. She must."

They both nodded, and then we parted ways. I packed my things for travel, and then I made my way to the healing tents. I had been there often of late. To see Kayla.

She wasn't in her room, so I searched for her in the healing tents. Perhaps she'd gone there for more medicine.

I did not expect to find my half-sister in a white bed, her skin paler than usual, her limbs weak from atrophy. The healer, Seri, stood over her, applying damp cloths to my sister's head.

"What is this?" I asked. "She was on the mend last I saw her. I was only gone a few days."

Seri gritted her teeth. "We found her like this in her bed. We cannot wake her."

I clenched my fist. "Why has she relapsed so suddenly? What did you give her, Fae? What?"

Fear appeared in her eyes. But then it passed, replaced with concern. "Nothing new. This must be a result of the concoctions the Prince of Envy gave her. They have assaulted her mind, driven her to hallucinations and madness. A relapse isn't out of the realm of possibility in a case like this."

"But she was doing better," I said, my voice loosing its thunder in grief and worry.

"She was running off a last burst of energy, my lord," said Seri. "But when it expired, her body shut down. She collapsed."

I looked at my sister, my dear sister who endured torture unspeakable. Torture that would have broken many I know. "When will she wake?"

"I do not know, my lord. She is fighting a difficult battle. A battle to regain her mind. It could take days. Weeks. Perhaps even longer."

My fist fell apart into a trembling hand. "But, she will wake, yes?"

Seri looked away, her eyes nervous. "It is possible, my lord. But it remains to be seen whether it is the Kayla you know who will wake, or another."

"No." I punched the wooden pillar to my side, breaking it in half and almost sending the tent falling upon us. But it held, supported by other beams. I looked at Kayla and thought of the story Varis told me, of his sister who was never the same. If only I had done differently. If only I had grown in my powers. Perhaps I could have ridden to Stonehill sooner. Perhaps I could have saved her.

Seri took my hand, rubbing it gently. "It is not your fault, my lord. You retook this city. You stopped the torture of Fae and Shade. And you saved Kayla from a fate worse than death. Because of you, she still stands a chance."

"Because of me..." I whispered. "It is because of me that this happened at all."

Then I pulled back my hand and left. It was on my way back to my quarters, when I passed the inn at the base of the castle, that I saw him.

Tavian Gray.

He sat at a table outside a tavern, drinking under the bright sun. Drinking. While my sister lay asleep unable to wake.

I stepped forward and knocked the cup from his hands. "How is it that you drink and find pleasure while Kayla suffers? How have you recovered so quickly from the tortures inflicted on you both?"

The Fae sighed, flicking back his thick dark hair. He was a massive man, coiled in muscle, larger than any Fae I'd ever seen, at least as large as me. "Your brother spent more time on her than he did on me," said Tavian. "I wish it were not so. I wish I had stopped him."

At his words, I calmed. It seemed we wished the same. "I heard you were leaving."

"I was," he said, picking his cup back up from the mud and refilling it from the flagon of ale on the table. "But then I heard she'd relapsed, and I couldn't leave her this way."

"Who is she to you?" I asked.

"A friend." He said no more.

"And who are you to her?"

"I do not know. Perhaps I will never know." He raised his cup in a toast. "To Kayla."

I nodded. "To Kayla."

Then I left the man to his drink and sorrows. I did not know him, and that worried me. But he was an enemy to Levi and a friend to Kayla. That would have to be enough.

As I walked back to the castle, I surveyed the repairs on the main hall. Winter had arrived, and that made the gathering of stone and wood harder than ever. Supplies were short and work slow. It would be a long time before Stonehill could be as it once was. Perhaps that was fitting. The place felt wrong without Arianna. Maybe it would only be put right when she returned.

"There." Dean's words pull me back to the present. Back to the cold and snow and search. "Look there." He points down the hill at something.

I follow his gaze down to piles of gray wood one could barely call houses. "A Fae village. So?"

"It's empty," says Dean. "Utterly empty."

I look again, and see that he is right. There is no sign of life, not outside the huts or within. There is not even a hint of prints in the snow. Strange. Like most things these days. But perhaps it is a clue.

We descend the snowy slope and scour the village for people. I find a wooden horse and a doll made of cloth, but I find no children. I find needle and string and a hammer for building, but I find none to use them. All I find is the smell. Like embers and ash. The smell of burning though there is no fire. The feel of smoke in my chest though the air is clear. Something unnatural happened here. Something dark.

When I come upon the village center, I notice something grey sticking out from the snow. A bone. I dig through ice and sheets of white until I find more. They make a circle. A circle of bones. And in the center, a carcass. A dead goat cut open. Baron howls into the cold wind, disturbed by the power that remains.

"A ritual took place here," I say, further examining the scene.

Dean hears me and jogs to my side. "You think the Fae cast a spell?"

"Perhaps," I say, finding strings and beads.

"They must have done something wrong. Conjured something that turned on them."

I shake my head. "This was a dark ritual. A blood sacrifice. Whatever these people conjured, they intended to do so."

Dean looks around, his eyes spooked. "So you mean, these Fae...these Fae are gone...because they sacrificed themselves?"

"I believe they knew the cost, yes." I stand, brushing my hands clean of snow.

"But why do it then? Why give your own life?"

I shrug. "Perhaps Metsi told them to. Perhaps she convinced them the sacrifice would win the war."

Dean scans the nearby houses. "So you think Metsi started this ritual. Why? For power?"

"Or knowledge." I walk around, searching for anything else unusual. "I have seen such rituals before, at the base of the Grey Mountain. Shamans would call for wisdom of the future. Sometimes, for the strength to defeat rival tribes. The Outlanders would always make a sacrifice to summon the power. The power they called the Darkness."

"And yet," says Dean, "in all my centuries of ruling, I have never seen this dark power."

"Your realm isn't on the outskirts," I say.

And then I see it.

Footprints.

Someone survived.

They ran.

I follow the tracks, Dean and Baron at my heels, until I reach a shack at the back of the village. I try the door and find it barred from within. So I smash it open. Inside, there is nothing but darkness. Nothing but shadow.

"Hello?"

A whimper. Weak. Fading.

"Hello?" I run in, looking, looking for the sound. "We mean you no harm. We only want to—"

Baron sniffs the air and runs forward. I follow, and I find her. I find the little girl crying in the corner, clutching a doll to her chest. I reach out to her. "We only want to help."

The girl doesn't move. She only looks up. Into my eyes. And she screams.

3

THE WRAITH

Fenris Vane

"There are monsters in the world, Arianna.
They are real. I am real."

—Asher

It takes hours to coax out the barest of details. But eventually, she opens up. Her name is Romana. Her father was the smith and her mother training to become the village elder. She would train one day as well. If things had gone differently.

"They came from the mountains," says the Fae girl, no older than ten, sitting by the fire, wrapping her arms around her legs. "They raided our village. Killed the butcher and stole our food and our jewels. Next few days, more of us died from hunger. We heard of more raids in the neighboring villages. The vampires were killing and taking all in their path. They said someone called Salzar led them. They said he was a monster with four arms and hooves for feet."

The girl trembles, and I wrap my cloak around her, keeping her sheltered from the cold. "Thank you," she whispers, her voice a soft, frail thing.

"Here," says Dean, passing her the roasted rabbit he caught and cooked earlier as I set up camp.

"Thank you." She puts the food to her mouth and nibbles slowly. After a moment, she seems to shake less, and her voice seems stronger. "After a few weeks, we started doing better, we did. Hunters brought in food again. And pa started forging weapons. In case the vampires came back." She looks up at us, as if remembering what we are. Then she looks back down at the food in her hands and bites her lip. "Are all vampires mean?"

"Not all," I say, stoking the campfire. "Some of us are good. Some of us less so."

The girl nods, knowingly. "So you're like us. You have good and bad people." Her eyes turn dark again. "The bad people kept raiding.

"They kept attacking the other villages, and our folk couldn't just stand by and let it happen. So they made a plan. I heard the Elder One tell my mother. They would perform a ritual, cast a plague upon the raiders. It would have a cost, she said. A big cost. And I was thinking maybe it cost a lot of money like the goats do. But mum told me it wasn't really like that. It was more like doing something nice for someone even if it wasn't too pleasant for yourself. Kind of like slowing down when we play Runner so the really young ones can keep up. Kind of like losing sometimes on purpose so they feel special. I hate losing."

She goes quiet after that. I don't prod her on. I don't do anything. The words will come in time. When she's ready.

Dean passes Romana another piece of meat, and she chews more vigorously than before. When she's done, she speaks. "I was playing out in the woods with my brother on the day of the ritual. We were supposed to be back by sun down, before the three moons be rising and turning full. He started to head back at the proper time, my brother did, but I wanted to stay and collect some flowers for mum. I lost track of things, and then, when I came back..."

Her lips tremble. Her eyes swell with tears.

"When I came back they were gone. All of them. And then I found the bones. All those bones. It was them. My mum and my pa. My brother..." Her words turn to sobs, and I wrap an arm around the girl, holding her close as I imagine Arianna would do. I make noises I hope are soothing.

Dean leans over and whispers in my ear. "You think this plague killed the raiders?"

"Maybe...but, the ritual would have needed a target. A campsite perhaps." I look at Romana. "Did anyone speak of where the raiders were staying? Where they were living?"

She nods, wiping tears off her face. "Down by the Raven Rock."

I caress the top of her head, smoothing her dark blue hair. "Do you know where that is?"

She nods.

"Can you take us there?"

She nods.

I stand, dusting snow off my clothes.

Dean grabs my arm. "And why are we going to this place where everyone is likely dead?"

"If there is a plague," I say, "we must make sure it is contained. Otherwise it may spread to Stonehill." I lower my voice so only he can hear. "And I do not believe that is the full of it. These villagers were taken by the Darkness. They didn't just die. Their power was absorbed by something."

Dean raises an eyebrow. "Metsi?"

I nod. "Varis told me she will do anything to win this war. He told me a madness has consumed her."

"So if we go to this Raven Rock, we might find Metsi. And if we find Metsi, we might find—"

"—Arianna," I finish.

We travel with renewed purpose, following the Fae girl through the darkness, carrying handmade torches. She has more energy than I would have expected, and she seems to fear the forests less than she feared her own village. She is now an orphan, homeless and parentless. If only Kayla would recover, she would know how to care for the girl. How to help her heal from this trauma. "It will be next to the river," she says, pointing forward to where a waterfall crashes down.

The sight makes me uneasy. Metsi is at her most powerful near the waves. But I do not suspect we will find her now. At most, we fill find a clue. A clue to where she may have gone.

When we come upon Raven Rock, I see that it is a cave. A perfect place to camp and hold out against the elements. Baron backs away from the opening, whining. Something seems to stir within.

A gust of wind hits us. And Romana clutches my leg. "It's here. The Darkness."

"Only the wind," I say, though I don't truly believe it. I glance at Dean. "Perhaps it best you stay out here with her."

He frowns. "And leave you to go in there alone? What if you do find Metsi? Or this...Darkness thing?"

I turn to Romana. "Baron will stay out here with you. Won't you boy?" His white head bobs between me and the girl, and I can sense his indecision. He doesn't want to leave me alone in the cave.

I kneel and pet his thick fur. "I'll be okay, boy. Take care of Romana. She needs you now. I'll be back shortly."

Baron reluctantly stays with the girl as Dean and I head into the cave.

Our torches are the only light, revealing walls of stone covered in markings. Runes I do not recognize. Drawings of beasts and men.

Dean studies the patterns, his jaw falling as he does. "This must have been an ancient dwelling. A place the Fae lived before they developed civilization."

I snicker. "Or these are just the ramblings of a mad man. An exile sent here to live out his days."

"An exile who knows ancient scripts?'

I shrug, carrying on until we reach something blocking our path. Roots thick and old.

Dean looks them over under the torchlight. "This would be no place for raiders. These roots are hundreds of years old."

I draw my sword. "Unless these roots grew here only after the ritual."

"You think," Dean says. "You think the Darkness made these?"

I nod. "Perhaps it has something to hide." I raise my sword and cut down, slicing through the roots. They fall away, groaning under my assault. I tell myself it is only the echoes, but the roots seem more sentient then I would like. I ignore their cries and cut until we are through their path. With the roots behind us, we step into a cavern, where the ceiling is breeched open, allowing moonlight to fall upon the ground. It is a memorizing sight, the light, dancing and twirling in the darkness. A moment later, I notice what hides in the shadows.

Bones. Hundreds of bones.

The remnants of a fire.

The whisper of broken blades.

And then, I see something that fits not at all.

I see a shelf of books. Old and engraved in ancient ruins. Yet, there is no dust upon them. They have been used. They have been maintained. Something has been living here.

And it was not the raiders.

A whine echoes behind me. Full of pain and agony. A whimper of an injured animal.

Baron!

I turn with haste.

And then I see her.

Cloaked in shadow.

Wisps of black smoke flowing off her body.

A black rag hanging over her eyes.

There is only one part of her not hidden to darkness. Her teeth. Bright and sharp. Too many of them, layered upon themselves. Too many to fit one mouth.

She smells like embers and ash. The smell of burning though there is no fire. The feel of smoke in my chest though the air is clear. I hadn't noticed before, but the scent only left me once. Only when we left the girl at the edge of the cave.

There was never a Fae child in the village. There was never a bandit camp.

There was only the Darkness.

The creature speaks. It has the voice of a youth. The voice of a little Fae girl. "The villagers were as easy to fool as you, Fenris. So quickly they rushed to perform my ritual, when I promised them safety and vengeance. So quickly did they sacrifice themselves."

The poor souls. She tricked them. Fooled them into casting a false ritual and absorbed their powers as her own. But why?

Dean draws his bow, knocking back an arrow. "What are you!" he yells.

The thing, the Wraith, laughs. She drifts through the air, moving slowly, then swifter than the eye can see. Behind my shoulder. Behind Dean's. Whispering in my ear. Whispering in his. When she speaks, her voice is young and old, light and dark all at once. "I am before your time, my prince. I was here when this world was new, and I will be here when it is old. You are but children to me." She runs a hand down my cheek. Vanishes. Appears before me. "Such sweet children."

She is still. And this is our chance.

Dean fires an arrow. I charge.

And then the world turns upside down.

I am no longer on the floor. I hang from the ceiling. Something holds my legs. Roots dark and thick. Dean hangs beside me.

The Wraith is still right side up, her face before me. "We will not fight, my young princes. That is not why I brought you here."

Here. This place of her power. This place where she can bind us and trap us with mere thoughts. This is why she lured us here. And I followed like a fool, when I should have been searching for Arianna.

I spit at the Wraith. "Then what? What do you want?"

She glides around us, sliding her hands over our bodies, tapping at us with long, sharp nails. "I have a proposition, my dear princes. There is someone I seek. Someone outside my power. Bring him to me."

Dean snickers. "And what? You'll let us go? Leave us alone?"

The Wraith speaks softly. "I will do more than that, my dear. I will tell you where you can find your princess. Where you can find Arianna."

I gasp at the mention of her name. At the chance. At hope. This cannot be true. But, if the Wraith has such power, she will know. She will know where I must go.

"Who?" I ask through gritted teeth. "Who is it that you want?"

She leans in. Her breath cold and freezing upon my cheek. And then she whispers his name. "Tavian Gray."

4

THE CHAIN THAT BINDS ME

Fenris Vane

"Fen is a good man, but he is myopic in his focus."
—Kayla Windhelm

I wake in the snow, gasping for breath, the sunlight blinding my eyes. Baron jumps to my side, licking at the frost on my hair. He appears uninjured. Whatever the Wraith did, he has recovered. For once, I am grateful he is a Spirit and no mortal wolf. Losing him…losing him is not something I can think of, so instead I pet his head, soothing his excitement. "Easy boy, I'm fine. I'm fine."

He puts his paws on my chest, as if to check for wounds, or perhaps just to be closer. For a moment, we just look into each other's eyes, man and animal, grateful we are both alive.

Then the snow next to me stirs, and Dean pushes out from underneath the layers of white. "What the bloody hell happened? What was that thing?"

"The Darkness," I say, memories returning to me. Memories of smoke and bone.

Dean looks around, then pauses, glancing at me. "You've seen it before, haven't you?"

"Once. At the Grey Mountain."

Dean nods. "Your trial. The one you had to pass to gain your own realm. You remember?"

I stand, turning away. "Bits and pieces. They return to me slowly ever since…" I cannot say the words. Not yet. Not even though I made stone move with my bare hands.

Dean finishes for me. "Ever since you learned you're Fae."

I nod. All the acknowledgement I can give. Then I return to the point. "I found her lair deep in the mountain, filled with bones and books. And then…"

"Then what?"

"I…I don't remember." Odd. The memory just ends. "I must have escaped. Then I made my way higher, to slay the Grey Beast."

Dean leans back, smiling. "Oh yes, those were the days. Back when there was still dangerous game to hunt."

I remember the snow-covered peak. The blizzard. The dark beast hidden in the torrent of wind and ice.

When I speak, my voice carries no happiness. "Yes... those were the days."

In some ways, I miss them. But it is a somber and wistful kind of missing. Back then, I was free. I had no realm. No great duty. I only had my father and brothers to please. Perhaps I should never have cared to please them. Perhaps then, I would still be free.

I study the sky, determining the time, around noon, and the stones, determining our location, not far from Stonehill. "We should go. The Waystone is nearby."

Dean jumps to his feet. "Think you misspoke, brother. We need to return to Stonehill. We need to find Tavian Gray."

My jaw clenches. "You'd make dealings with the Wraith?"

"I would do anything for Arianna," he says, his voice soft but strong. "Anything."

So would I. But to sacrifice a man I barely know to a fate unknown..."Tavian has caused us no harm."

"But he is no friend either. What do we even know of him?"

I remember back to the days when we first reclaimed Stonehill. "He's friend to Kayla."

Dean scoffs. "So he says."

"So she says. I saw her with him before she passed out."

Dean curls his fingers, his voice laced with venom. "So she says after torture and drinking poisons. For all we know, he could be the reason she suffers in the first place."

"I do not think so," I say, remembering my talk with Tavian outside the tavern. "Why would he stay then? Why would he stay unless to see her recovered?"

Dean rubs his chin. "Hmm, I don't know, maybe so he can kill her if she does wake? Or perhaps he has other motives. Maybe he's a spy for the Fae. Maybe that's why he hangs around Stonehill."

He makes good points. I know so little of Tavian. But it doesn't mean I can't find out.

"We will try the Waystone first," I say.

Dean rolls his eyes. "Even if the Waystone works, we still don't know where to look for her. If what you say is true, Avakiri is as large as Inferna. Where would we even start?"

He is right, but I must try to find another way. I cannot condemn a man before exhausting all other options. Nor can I make a deal with the Darkness unless it's truly my only option. I don't have a good feeling about this. "We try the Waystone first," I say, and then I lead the way, never glancing back at my brother.

His footsteps let me know he follows, but we do not speak. Not for a long time. I know he scorns following my lead. I do not blame him. I would scorn him, if roles were reversed. We are demons of power and influence, with lives longer than any human can imagine. We were not bred to be followers, even of each other.

Eventually, Dean speaks. "I suppose I need the practice, for when you're king and all."

"I won't be king," I say instantly.

He scoffs. "Oh, yes you will. When Arianna gives you an heir."

"Arianna and I, we haven't...we won't..." I stop, looking at Dean. He has guilt all over his face. "What did you do?"

He smacks his lips. "Remember the night of the celebration? Right before we marched? Well...I may have slipped you a love potion."

"You what?"

He jumps back like a startled animal. "It doesn't affect those already in love, but it can give one a push in the right direction."

"You mean Arianna and I? You mean, this is why I can't remember that night?"

"Yeah. Probably."

My fist slams into his face, sending him flying.

He tumbles through the snow, stopping near a tree. He sits up against the trunk, rubbing his jaw. "Ah, so this is how Asher feels." He glances at me. "Trust me, I did you a favor."

I storm up to him, kicking snow in my wake, as Baron growls at Dean. "A favor? You twisted my mind, robbed me of my ability to choose."

"Because you were taking too bloody damn long!"

I raise my fist again. "Why would you do this? Don't you want to be king?"

He sighs, looking away. And I see the playfulness leave him. "I want this to be over. I want to know she can never pick me. Because right now, while there is still a chance, I still hope. And hope brings only pain when it is a false hope. I just want to be free, brother. I just want to be free of her."

I lower my hand, some of my rage leaving me. "Then choose to be free, brother. Choose to be free and move on."

He stares back at me, his eyes glistening. "Don't you see Fenris? I did move on. In my own way."

I sigh. "And what a foolish way. A love potion. It was only one time then. Arianna is likely not pregnant."

The guilty face returns. "Well, you see, I may have slipped her a potion as well."

"No."

"A potion that almost guarantees—

"It can't be—"

"Almost guarantees pregnancy."

I punch him again.

Harder.

And then I fall to my knees and yell. "How dare you do this? How dare you condemn me to a life of servitude?"

Dean flinches. "Servitude? Brother, you will be king."

"You know I will be a slave to the crown."

He stands, adjusting his jaw. "Well, in that case, we are all slaves, aren't we? You. Me. Asher. So why not be the slave in charge of everything? The slave who can actually change things in this forsaken world? A slave who gets to love the woman we all want? The woman who loves you in return."

I turn away from him, shock consuming my body. "She may not be pregnant. She may not be pregnant. She may—"

"Oh, she bloody damn well is man. Get over it. And go save your woman and your child."

I charge him, grabbing him by the collar and pinning him against the tree. "You idiotic, meddling fool!"

I expect Dean to fight back but he slumps in defeat in my arms. "I had no other choice. I don't know any other way to get over her, to end this constant torment I feel. She only wants you."

I let him go. My breath is heavy. I try to calm it. "I didn't need your help. I would have gotten there eventually. On my own."

"That seems...unlikely. You had her for a whole month and made zero progress. Admit it, you need your brother of lust every now and then to keep things going."

I chuckle. Despite everything I chuckle. Perhaps I'm going mad.

I laugh some more, feeling the shock and anger drain from me. Feeling a kind of peace at knowing I no longer have to choose between Arianna and freedom. The choice has been made for me. Of course, I would have rather decided myself. But still. There is peace in having choice taken away. Even if it is a fool's peace.

Before I become enraged once more, I turn, Baron at my heel, and continue on to the Waystone. "Time to get some more practice following me, brother."

Dean laughs as he runs to catch up.

I focus on my goal and try to keep thoughts away. Thoughts of Arianna. Thoughts of our child. Thoughts of being king.

It's dusk by the time we arrive at the cave with the Waystone, the cave where I searched for Arianna before. I place my hand upon the great stone door, and a needle pierces my flesh, letting my blood flow into the carvings. This time, I am a Druid. This time, it must work.

The door does not move.

I push my hand harder onto the needle, squeezing out more blood.

Nothing.

Dean sits on a rock, his eyes dark. "There is only one thing left, then."

I try to find an argument to sway us both, but there is none. Arianna comes above all. Above Tavian Gray's life. Above any reservations I feel about making deals with the Darkness. "We will speak with him first," I say.

Dean nods.

And then we head for Stonehill.

The city is carved into a mountain, filled with raging waterfalls and glowing crystals protruding from the stone. Past the large gates, small buildings of wood and stone line the cobble streets. Deeper into the city, the architecture grows more grand, the use of stone more common and exquisite. Deeper still stands the castle, a mass of gray rock built from the mountainside. It rises into the pale cloudy sky, looming over the thousands of people below, reminding them of their ruler, of their kingdom, of their duty. It is a marvel of architecture, art and nature converging.

And it is the chain that binds me.

I push away thoughts of responsibility as we pass the market square, the stage where Fae are bought and sold. None are on show today. But still people crowd this part of the city, gathering at stalls, bartering for goods, bidding for services. Their voices muddle together, but one catches my attention.

"You forget your place, Fae," says a man as he smashes his fist into his slave, knocking her into the mud. Thick robes and heavy jewelry swing from his person, while the Fae wears only tattered gray rags. He grabs her ear, twisting it, and she squeals in pain. "How dare you forget to bring my cane? I will—"

I flick my hand, and the earth beneath the man shifts. He falls to the ground, staining his white robes in the brown dirt. Gasping, he looks around, his face flushed red. Hiding his embarrassment, he covers his face and tries to stand, only to fall again, this time kissing the mud with his lips.

Dean glances my way. "Careful, brother."

I shrug, my lips curling into a smile. "The man is clumsy. I didn't make him so." And in truth, I didn't mean to do as I did. My powers are more instinct than plan. When I rushed in front of Arianna, jumping between her and the flames, when I threw my arms up in defense, all I sought was to protect her with my body. I did not expect to move the very earth with my will, and yet I did. What to make of that I still don't know. Should I train as Varis suggests? But how? How could I find the time when I must first find Arianna?

Dean shakes his head at my silence, sighs, and says nothing as we make our way for the castle. We pass the wooden poles and crosses raised by Levi's men. They are empty now, the Fae pulled down and buried by my command. But still they stand as a reminder of innocent blood spilled. When I can spare the men, I should have them pulled from the earth, but for now my workers toil at the castle, repairing the wall destroyed by Levi's explosives. I did not think he would risk the lives of so many innocents to set a trap for Arianna. What a fool I was.

When we pass the gates, and enter the great hall, half majestic, half charred and broken, I find my Keeper, Kal'Hallen overseeing the repairs. "Find Tavian Gray. I must have words with him."

"Of course, my lord," says the ancient Fae, stepping forward and clutching his stomach; he has still not fully recovered from his wound. "When shall I have him meet you?"

I walk to the tree at the center of the hall, up the stairs that will lead to my room. "Tonight."

The Keeper swallows hard, unease in his eyes. "But my lord, what of the ball?"

I freeze. "What ball?"

"Oh dear. I thought Prince Asher had consulted you—"

"What ball?"

He licks his lips. "In your absence, my lord, your brother planned a ball for this evening."

Dean and I exchange a look. Asher is overstepping. "Tell him I will not attend," I say, growling, "It is what he expects anyway."

I turn away, walking up stairs, and Kal hurries behind me. "My lord, I think that would be unwise. He will be here, after all."

I stop, dread twisting my stomach. "Who?"

"Your brother, my lord. Prince Niam."

5

PRINCE OF GREED

Fenris Vane

"Don't let the pretty baubles fool you, Princess. We are still demons. This is still a dangerous place."

—Fenris Vane

My fist smashes into Asher's face.

He flies through the air, slamming into the wall of his chambers and falling to the ground. He rubs his chin, and Dean, who stands beside me, does the same in some strange sympathetic gesture. I glance between them, bewildered. Then focus back on Asher. "How dare you not consult us?"

He shrugs, still sitting on the floor by his bed. "You were busy searching for Arianna. In fact, I'm curious as to why you have returned? I don't see the princess."

"We…" I pause, deciding not to give too much away to my treacherous brother. "We need to gather more supplies."

"I see," says Asher. "Well, just as you need supplies, I need security. That is why I summoned Niam. To discuss peace."

I clench my fists. "Peace? He voted to have Arianna and I killed! What kind of peace can I make with him?"

"You alone? None. But the three of us together…" He stands, dusting off his suit. "Though most of our brothers hate you and dislike me, they have a fondness for Dean. And no matter their opinion, we have power. There are three of us. Four of them—three since Levi is yet to be found. Almost an equal split of the Seven Realms. If they challenge us, they start a full on civil war. A war that will tear the land apart even without help from the Fae."

Dean nods. "If Niam agreed to attend, he must be interested in discussing a treaty. And if we can get Niam, he'll get us the others."

"Exactly," says Asher. "And we will make sure it is a treaty that benefits both parties. A treaty that keeps peace while you two go about searching for the Princess."

I don't like the idea of meeting Niam, but I see no other alternatives. Still…"A ball? Could it not have been a council meeting? You know I am not made for such things, and the timing hardly seems appropriate. We have our realms to rebuild and a possible war to plan for. Not to mention Arianna to find. This isn't the time for a party."

Asher studies me up and down. "Not everyone shares your distaste for the finer things in life, brother. And a ball is exactly the setting we need for a talk of peace. Wine, women, music…some much needed distraction after so much stress. You must learn to alleviate the pressure when it builds, lest it explode in your face. This will remind our brothers of the perks of a united family. So, off with you. Prepare for the festivities. Make sure to clean yourselves up. And find something nice to wear. You look like savages."

Dean chuckles, I sigh, Baron growls, and then we return to our own rooms. In moments, my servants, two Fae girls, dress me in silks. Pale blues and a white vest. A tight collar and tighter cuffs. Bloody hell. How does Asher stand such clothing?

When they are done dressing me like a doll, I leave for the grand hall, sweating below the many layers of clothing designed to torture men. I try to ignore the discomfort. Ignore the knowledge that every moment I spend at this ball is a moment stolen from my search for Arianna. And when I see the ballroom, full of dancing and drinking, of laughter and smiles, I wish Arianna were here. I wish it was we who were dancing. We who were laughing.

I think of the night before we went to battle. The night I thought I'd forgotten from alcohol. The night I made love to Arianna for the first time. It's not a night she'll have likely forgotten, which means I am a complete ass, because the following day we barely talked.

I have to find her. Have to make it up to her. Have to explain…everything.

Soon, I vow. Soon.

Someone brushes past me. A woman wearing a golden dress, her black hair twisted in a complex bun, surely to impress the other nobles. Her skin is pale and perfect and her smile bright. A masquerade mask of silver feathers covers her face. "Would my lord care for a dance?"

"Perhaps later," I say, trying to be delicate. Of course what I really mean is perhaps never.

I make my way through the room, politely refusing all advances, Baron at my side, growling at anyone who pushes too far. When Asher sees the wolf, he rolls his eyes. "Really? You couldn't leave him at home?"

"This *is* my home," I say, smirking. "If you don't like Baron, you can leave."

Baron bares his teeth in agreement, and Asher backs away. "No. No. I'm fine, dear brother." He pats my vest, adjusting my collar. "Just, when the others arrive, don't do anything rash, okay? We seek peace, not war."

"Then you have the wrong prince," I say, ruffling my collar back to how it was. "When can we expect Niam?"

Asher shrugs. "Seems he's running late."

I scan the ballroom, noticing the woman in gold again. She dances with a man in white, the masquerade mask on his face matching her own. They switch partners as the flow of music hastens, and all the dancers move in intricate patterns. Dean is on the dance floor, wearing a vest and pants, nothing more, his golden chest oiled and glistening under the swirling lights. He laughs, flirts, drinks and dances. Seems he's well on his way to getting over Arianna, but I do wonder... how deep do his feelings go for her? Deeper than he's letting on, I think. And for a moment I feel sorry for him. I realize that with Arianna he could have it all, and yet she wants me, a man who wants nothing to do with these political machinations. It's amazing he doesn't hate me for that alone.

A servant offers me roasted pork on a platter. "No, thank you," I say, preferring to get my own food. Though perhaps I am just sick of slaves catering to my every whim. To all our whims. The vampires live with too much leisure. The Fae with too much servitude.

Speaking of Fae...

Varis approaches me as Asher walks off to dance. The Fae looks wearier than he did, but he smiles brightly. "Finally, some decent company," he says.

"Any news of Arianna?"

He shakes his head, pouring himself a drink that glows purple. "There has been no sign of her. Not even whispers."

I clench my jaw, not surprised, but frustrated all the same. "What of Metsi?"

"She seems to have hidden herself away as well," says Varis, sighing. "What of you? Any luck?"

I lower my voice. "We did find a creature. A Wraith shrouded in darkness. She vowed to tell us of Arianna's location, if..."

Varis's eyes go wide. The wind around him begins to stir. "If? If what?"

I glance around, noticing Tavian by the bar, lost in drink. "If we deliver someone to her."

Varis follows my gaze. "The traveler?"

I nod. "What do you know of him?"

"I have heard tales of his deeds, but how many of them are true I cannot say. He is one of the older ones though, that is certain."

I raise an eyebrow, studying the large man at the bar that is Tavian Gray. "Older ones? Older than you?"

Varis nods, a severity to his look.

I can't make sense of this. Not from what I know. "But he looks as old as Kayla. His hair isn't even white yet."

"There are ways to color hair, Fenris," says Varis.

True. But I have never seen a Fae do so. Age is a symbol of respect in their culture, so none seek to hide theirs.

Varis takes another drink, shivering from the strong effects. "This creature you spoke of. It seems of—"

"The Darkness," I say. "It is."

Varis grabs my arm, his voice taut with urgency. "Then you cannot make dealings with it. The Midnight Star tapped into the Darkness back in the Moonlight Garden, and the grove of my ancestors burned as a result. Innocents were injured. The city nearly ruined."

"I am aware," I say, pulling my arm away and pouring a drink for myself. I put the cup to my lips, pretending to sip so others would see me at ease. But I do not drink. I must keep my wits about me. "I am as loathe to deal with the Wraith as you, but what are we to do then? We have no leads."

"Something may yet present itself. In the meantime, have you given more thought to—"

"Yes," I say, recalling our talks over the past weeks. "And the answer is still no. I do not have time to train."

Varis raises his voice over our hushed whispers. "Your powers will grow whether you train or not. One day, you will lose control."

"What do you expect me to do?" I gesture at the ball. At the frivolous festivities that waste my time. "I must find Arianna. Every part of me must be focused on this task. Without her, nothing will matter. Nothing."

"I know," says Varis, dropping his gaze to the floor. "But have you considered what you will do *when* you find her? Metsi is no weak foe. She has the Water Spirit on her side. She has an army of Fae willing to die in fanaticism. And she knows how to use her powers to full effect. What do you have?"

I glance at Baron and pat his head. "I have defeated Wadu before."

"I heard. But that was only the Spirit. Fighting both Spirit and Druid at once is another matter entirely. Not to mention the army she wields. And as I recall, you did not fare well against Oren..."

Oren. The Fire Druid who nearly killed me. The reason my powers awakened. "I will find a way to defeat Metsi," I say, turning away, not wishing to discuss this further.

Varis sighs again. "Please, let me teach you at least—"

Something catches my eye. The man in white. The one in the mask. He's no longer dancing. Instead, he reaches into his vest. In the blink of an eye, he draws a dagger.

And throws it at Varis.

There is no time to think. To plan. Only instinct drives me. The instinct of battle. Of survival. I dash forward, flinging my arm into the air. And I catch the dagger by the handle. A foot from the Druid's face. For a moment, he is not even aware of the happenings around him. For a moment, he is still finishing his sentence to me. But then he notices what has transpired. And his face fills with dread.

Someone claps. The man in white.

"As fast as ever, brother," he says, his voice smooth and thick. "Maybe even faster." He pulls off his mask, revealing his bald head and pristine dark skin, and walks over to join us, sitting at the table.

Niam.

I point his own dagger at his chest. "How dare you assault my guest?"

He shrugs casually. "How dare you harbor a Druid? As I see it, things now stand equal."

Scales and balances. That is what Niam is. The Prince of Greed. The Prince of Wealth. His white robes glitter under the flickering lights. Gold buttons run down his vest, and a sapphire adorns his neck. His smile is charming, perhaps even seductive to some. He appears as a friend, a close confidant I can trust, even after all he has done. That is the way with Niam. People always seek to be his friend, his ally, even as he stabs them in the back. Even I, for a moment, forget his true nature. But then I remember. He is my enemy, even though he comes as my guest.

"Why the charade?" I ask, gesturing at the mask in his hand as I return to my seat across from him. We are apparently playing this casual. I can do casual. More or less.

"Oh this?" he holds up his mask. "Just a bit of fun. A chance to see Stonehill as a common man. I do the same in my realm you know. Walk the streets and inspect the stalls under the guise of a traveler. You learn so much about the people this way, of what they truly think of their rulers." He grabs an apple from a platter and takes a big loud bite. I notice everyone is staring at us, anticipating what we will do next. Niam points at me. "They like you, the people. Even though you are a prince, even though you are a Druid, somehow, they relate to you. They praise you for driving away Levi. Some even admire your strict feeding regulations. They call for change, they do. And that is what they see you as. A symbol of change." He puts his feet up on one of the banquet tables. "We could use this to our advantage."

"We?" I chuckle at his delusion.

"We," he says, smiling, his teeth bright and perfect. "Why not? With Levi out of the picture, as it were, I need a new ally."

"You turn so easily?"

He looks surprised. "Don't we all? I recall a time not so long ago when we were allies, just before Arianna arrived to this bloody world. Perhaps we can put aside our differences once again. Not allow a woman to get in between brothers."

"What do you propose?" I do not truly seek an alliance, but I do need peace while I search for Arianna.

"Your realm is in disarray," he says plainly. "Between the raid from the Outlanders, the Fae battle, and Levi's occupation, your people have suffered and your goods have withered. You need wood and stone to repair your very castle. You need food to feed your people through the winter. I can provide all. In exchange for a small service."

Right. Niam doesn't know the meaning of the word small. "What service?"

"Your help. And your army." He takes another bite of his apple. "With Levi missing, I seek to...secure... his realm."

I snicker at the audacity. "You mean conquer it?"

"I mean save. For without a proper ruler it will fall into chaos soon enough. Levi's men however, do not wish to give away their power. His generals squabble over Crimson Castle even as we speak."

"You have an army," I say, waving the dagger in my hand. "Take the castle yourself."

Niam rubs his chin. "I could, but many would fall in the battle. With your forces aligned with mine, perhaps even Dean's and Asher's as well, we could force them to surrender. No bloodshed."

Damn him. He knows I don't want to see innocent men fall. And he knows we need resources to recover from recent events. Niam is self-serving, but he's not stupid and he knows the value of things. Yet it is he who plans the battle. "What of Ace and Zeb? They turn on you already?"

He smacks his lips. "No. But Ace is staying neutral, as he calls it. And Zeb, well, Zeb does not wish to take Crimson Castle in case Levi returns. He thinks it would reflect poorly on him."

"But you just don't care what people think, don't you?"

His voice is cold when he speaks. "What people think is often irrational and changes on a whim. So no. I do not care. I would much rather spend my time getting results. Thoughts can easily be influenced later." He takes another bite of the apple. "So, what do you say? Should we discuss the details?"

I think over his offer. It would mean warm bellies and shelter for my people. It would mean faster repairs for my castle. It would mean less bloodshed in the south. But in the end, it would mean a deal with the devil.

I face my brother. And then I leap into the air and land on the table. Plates shatter under my heel and the table shakes and groans beneath my boots. I walk forward, kicking dishes and meals away, until I stand over Niam, glaring down at his small form below.

"I will not help you," I say, my voice stern, a voice you do not interrupt. "But you will help me. You will send your goods north, to Stonehill. You will send your supplies. And you will do so promptly."

Niam chuckles, but the humor doesn't touch his eyes. "And why would I do such a thing?"

"Because if you do not, I will throw you to the floor of this hall. I will punch those pretty teeth until they fall out red and bloody. And I will drag you to my dungeon. Where you will stay for all eternity."

He stands from his chair, his face filled with rage. "You wouldn't dare. I am your brother. I am your guest."

I kneel down, meeting him at eye level. "And perhaps that would count for something, if you hadn't tried to have your brother killed. If you hadn't attacked his guest in his very own hall. Perhaps then, it would count. But who knows? I never really liked you anyway."

"You...You..." Spittle flies from his mouth as he searches for the words. "You will not threaten me."

I grip the dagger in my hand. His dagger. And I put it against his throat. "I think you misunderstand. I don't make threats, brother. I am the Prince of War, or have you forgotten? I only make promises."

"I..." His eyes race around the room, surely searching for a way out. A way to safety. He seeks his guards, dressed in masks, planted throughout the room. But I spotted them early on and had their drinks spiked in anticipation of his arrival. They are sleeping off their drugged state in guarded rooms. He will find no ally, no help. He underestimates my capacity to anticipate danger and plan for it. I may not relish my title as Prince of War, but I have earned it and I do not wear it lightly. The cocky bastard should have thought ahead. But that is the way with Niam. People always like him, even when he stabs them in the back. Why should he worry? He just forgot, I'm no person. Not truly. I gave a part of myself away, a part of my humanity, when I took the throne. When I became half person, half prince. Half human, half duty. When I became the Prince of War. The Prince of Death.

I push the dagger into his skin, drawing a drop of blood.

Niam hisses, shutting his eyes. "Fine. Very well. I will send you the provisions you require. Now let me go."

"Seems you forget your own rules, brother," I say, twisting the dagger against his flesh. "Nothing is final until one signs a contract." I gesture at Asher who stands with a cup of wine. "Draw him up a contract, won't you? And quickly."

The Prince of Pride nods, fumbling to find parchment and paper. Eventually, a servant brings him some and he writes up the details. Wood, stone and food for my people. Nothing for Niam—except his safe return home. And he promises no retaliation for this agreement. The final thorn.

He lays the parchment on the table. And I shove a pen into Niam's hand. "Sign."

He breathes deeply, biting his own lip. Then, slowly, as if resisting with every muscle, he shoves the pen's sharp edge into his arm, drawing blood. His signature is hurried, but binding. A swirl of magic seals the contract, and I see the compulsion of his commitment weighing on him even now. He will not rest until he has fulfilled his bargain.

"We have a deal," I say, grinning, letting the dagger fall to my side.

Niam reaches for his neck, checking the injury. "You will not like the outcome, I assure you."

I cock my head, taking his measure, and smile. "Why don't I believe you?"

He wipes away the blood on his neck with a cloth napkin from the table and straightens his clothing. "I wasn't going to tell you, not if we had struck a bargain, but Zeb and Ace wish Levi returned."

I shrug. "Then they should speak to the Fae. Metsi is the one who likely holds him."

"Yes. But the way they see it—the way we all see it—you are responsible. You attacked him. And in the midst of the chaos you created, he was captured."

I stand back up, and hop off the table, laughing at this madness. "The chaos I created? I was reclaiming my own realm."

"Even so, it is on your head whatever happens to Levi. So, on behalf of Ace and Zeb and myself, I must inform you, you have one month. One month to return our dear brother, the Prince of Envy. And if you do not, we will invade. With all our forces. We will not stop until you are in chains, and those you love dead in the mud."

He turns, walking to the door. "Next time we see each other, my brother, I will be the one with the dagger. And you the one who is forced into submission."

6

I AM THE
PRINCE OF WAR

Fenris Vane

"One goblet contained poisoned wine. And how my father answered my questions would determine which goblet he received."

—Fenris Vane

The ball continues. Though admittedly with less joy than before. Asher stands at my side, tugging at his clothes in distracted annoyance. "You ruined our chance for peace! What am I supposed to do now? How am I supposed to prepare for war when we have barely any men to repair the fortifications?"

I pat his shoulder. "You'll find a way."

Dean nods, standing to my other side and drinking a purple wine. "We do have a month. Should be enough time to find Arianna and Levi, maybe even defeat Metsi and end the war. Hell, I don't even know what you're worried about." I know his tone is meant to lighten the mood, but no one laughs.

I grab both of them by the shoulders. "How about you two discuss plans? I have other business to attend to."

Asher's jaw drops. "Other business? What kind of other—"

I'm not listening. Already, I'm walking away from them. There is only one person left I must speak with tonight.

I find Tavian at the bar, a tankard of ale to his lips. He looks paler than he did before, more fragile somehow. These last few days have taken a toll on him. A toll on us all.

I push the thoughts away. I cannot stand to have empathy right now. I take the seat beside him and glare into his eyes. "What would a traveler know of a Wraith?"

Tavian takes another sip of his drink. "You speak in riddles, your *grace.*"

I tap my fingers on the wooden counter, my hand curled like a claw. "Then let me be clear. I just received an offer. Trade you for Arianna's location. Every part of my being wills me to accept. Every part but one. The part that whispers, what would Arianna do? I think she would give you a chance. See why this thing wants you. And then she would make her decision."

Tavian leans back, looking off into the distance. "You call it a thing. Not a man. Not a woman. A thing."

He pauses. "I know what you speak of. A creature cloaked in shadow. Wreathed in smoke."

"What does it want with you?"

"Many years ago, my colleagues and I performed a ritual. We sought to tap into a power thought uncontrollable."

"The Darkness," I whisper.

Tavian nods. "It answered our summons. And in the process destroyed everything I love. But three of us it left untouched—well, not untouched, but alive at any rate. Me and two others. Now it...searches for me. Searches so it can end what it began."

There was something to what he said. A pause that makes me think he is holding back. "This Wraith," I say, "is there a way to fight it?"

"No. You can only run. Run as I have." He does not offer more, but I see the weariness in him. The weariness of a man whose life is not his own. In this too, we are alike. Slaves to an outside force.

All because of one moment. One mistake.

"Will you leave once she recovers?" I ask. I see it in his face, he knows of who I speak. The one person who seems to matter to him most.

Kayla.

He nods. A sorrow in his eyes. "I have made it a habit to avoid the politics of this world, and when she wakes, her life will be nothing but political."

His words make no sense. "What do you mean?"

"Oh, of course." He chuckles. "You would not know. But I should not be the one to tell you."

"Tell me what?"

"When Kayla wakes, you will know. And if she doesn't wake, then I suppose it doesn't matter. None of it will have mattered."

I am tired of these games. These half-spoken truths. "Now who is the one speaking in riddles? You are not my friend, Tavian Gray. You are but a means to an end. Do not test me."

He shrugs. "I will not betray Kayla's trust. Would you do any differently?"

"I…" My words leave me. For he is right. I would not betray Kayla. And hurting this man, sacrificing this man, would be a betrayal above others. And even Varis urged against doing the bidding of the Darkness, a warning I do not take lightly.

"So, do I have to be worried?" I ask with a raised eyebrow.

He eyes me cautiously. "Worried?"

"When I don't deliver you to the Wraith, will it come after me?"

He shrugs. "Perhaps. But she is strongest in places of power. She will try to lure you to one before she attacks."

Places like Raven Rock. "So, I just need to avoid following strangers. Seems easy enough."

"She may not always appear as a stranger." There's a dread in his words. A primal fear.

And then someone slams two tankards down in front of us.

Dean.

"Why so gloomy, boys? Oh, wait, wait, I know. It's because you're not drinking. Drink." He sits down at the table with us and gulps down the syrupy liquid.

I suppose with Niam gone, I can indulge a bit. I raise my tankard to Tavian. "For Kayla."

He clanks his cup to mine. "For Kayla."

We drink.

And then we drink some more.

Eventually, I lose count.

And Tavian and I begin to speak more openly. "I heard you slayed a Dreadclaw," says the Fae. "What a battle that must have been."

Dean looks puzzled. "Dreadclaw?"

"He means the Grey Beast," I say.

Tavian shrugs. "Grey Beast. Dreadclaw. Different names from different places, but the thing is the same. Please, you must tell me the tale."

"Well, I—"

"He doesn't speak of it," says Dean. "But my brothers and I all know the legend. Fenris scaled the Grey Mountain with nothing but a spear. And at the top, he found the Grey Beast, its body more bone than flesh, its breath cold as ice. The beast charged my brother. And then Fenris leaped into the air. Like a devil he flew with the winds. And then he rammed his spear into the monster's head. In one single blow did the great beast fall. And Fenris stood untouched."

Tavian's eyes go wide. "Amazing. Did it truly happen like this?'

"More or less," I grumble, not wanting to go into the very real and different details. "How about we…" My words slur more than usual. My head grows fuzzy.

Something is wrong.

I try to stand, but instead I fall forward, my face slamming into the counter. I look up. At Tavian. His eyes glaze over. He falls.

Only Dean stands tall. Dean. Who gave us the drinks.

"I'm sorry, brother, but I knew you would never approve. It will seem as if you fell asleep from too much drink. You will wake here shortly. But Tavian is coming with me."

…

I am in dreams. In a land where there is no earth beneath my feet. No horizon before my eyes. My body feels ethereal. There is a lightness to my being. A lightness I have felt once before.

And she is there.

Radiant. Glowing.

Her white hair flicking in a wind I do not feel.

She hums a tune I recognize. Sad and lonely.

When she looks at me, she makes no sound, and yet I hear her words.

You are my heir.

The heir. The heir. The heir.

Her voice is not alone.

And when she turns, stepping aside, I see him. A figure in shadow.

I reach for him.

And I whisper.

"Father?"

...

"No!" I roar, jumping to my feet in the ballroom, the table before me disheveled from my violent reemergence into the world of the conscious.

Dean stumbles back, his eyes wide and bewildered. He drops Tavian to the ground. The people around us, the vampires dressed in gowns and the Fae dressed in slave's outfits freeze, turning to us, waiting to see what happens next.

"Impossible," Dean whispers. Then he raises his arms in surrender. "Now, now, brother. I was only doing what needed to be done. For Arianna. For all of us. So how about we calm down?"

It is because he asks me to be calm that I let rage fill me. I am tired of being told how to be. Tired of Dean controlling me with his potions. Tired of Asher trying to tell me how to rule. Tired of Niam trying to force my hand. So no. I will not be calm. I am the Prince of War.

I charge forward, grabbing Dean by the throat and pinning him against a wall. "You will not drug me again, brother. Nor will you touch Tavian. Or your fate will be the same one I promised Niam."

He squirms in my grip, clutching at his throat. "I… fine. I promise. I won't."

I let go. And he falls to the ground, coughing and spitting.

I turn to my other brother. Asher. "And you. You do not rule in my stead. You do not throw parties I do not allow. You do not invite princes I have not approved. Do you understand?"

He nods, adjusting his collar, sweat running down his forehead.

I turn away from them both and grab a torch from the walls. I head to the door.

"Where are you going?" asks Asher.

I do not answer. Instead, I make my way out the gate, down the steps, my torch lighting the night, my gaze focused forward, my steps steady. Guests follow me, perhaps curious to see where I go, perhaps ready to leave as well. They gather behind me, joined by people from the street. Dozens, then hundreds. They follow me as I reach the square where stand the wooden poles and crosses. Where stand the symbols of depravity.

And I burn them down.

"Heed me," I roar into the night, into the heavens above. "None will live at the whims of others anymore. We will be free. Free to do as we wish. From now on..." I turn to the crowd, to the thousands of slaves gathered there. "From now on...the Fae will be free."

The crowd cheers. And I think back to when I first became a ruler, when I returned from Grey Mountain and became the Prince of War. It has been often on my mind of late. Why? Is it because...and then I remember who brought it up: Lucian. He remembered it well. How? Why? Unless...Unless he had been there recently.

I turn to my brothers and tell them. "I know where Arianna is."

7

REBORN

"Let's just say there's pain involved. Lots of pain."

—Asher

I wake slowly on a soft linen bed, my eyes hazy, my mouth dry. And then I remember. Levi attacking me. Draining me. I remember his teeth penetrating my neck. I felt Yami panic, his magic pounding against a cage he couldn't free himself from. And I remember… dying.

My hands drop to my belly, fear taking hold of me. My baby? Is my baby okay?

"You are both fine," says a deep voice.

I see him then, sitting by the bed, clad in black, his dark hair streaked with grey. He watches me with cold blue eyes. His face is hard. It reminds me of Fen and Asher, and so I look away.

"Why are you here, Lucian?" I ask, my voice weak and hoarse, my mouth filled with cotton balls, my head spinning and aching.

From the corner of my eye I see him smile, teeth white and perfect. "Is it so hard to believe? You've known from the start I've been working with the Fae. Right now, that means helping Metsi."

I force myself to face him, to glare into his eyes. "You don't care about the Fae. You told me yourself."

He shrugs. "I say many things. Who's to say which are true?"

He won't fool me. I remember. I remember he cares nothing for the Fae. And then I remember his promise. His promise that he will come for me.

"So is this it?" I ask. "Is this when you take your revenge on me?"

He pauses, then chuckles. "Oh no. Quite the contrary. I came here to help you."

"Help me?" More memories come flooding in. Losing blood. Falling. Fading. "What happened?" I ask, sitting up. The motion pains me, but not as much as I expected. "I remember—"

"Dying? You did." Lucian grins. "I brought you back. Both of you."

Like he did before. Like he did when I died as a child. When my mother made a deal with the devil. "Did someone offer you their soul this time too?"

He grabs an apple from a platter next to my bed and takes a bite. "Metsi did promise me a favor, but in truth, she needn't have. You are useful to me, you see."

Him and his games. I'm tired of them. "How long? Since I died."

"A few days." He shrugs as he chews the apple. "Not long, in the grand scheme of things, though the world keeps spinning, and inexplicably so much of it continues to revolve around you."

"What do you want from me?"

"You will see soon enough."

Lies. Secrets. I'm used to them now, but Lucian worries me. More than Metsi. More than Oren did. Around Lucian, I feel a dread, thick and oozing. It pours into me, makes me tremble and sweat.

I clutch the bed sheets closer to stay warm. "What are you, really?"

He looks puzzled, though it seems in mockery. "A vampire, of course."

"You have powers no other vampire seems to possess. Bringing people back from the dead."

He stands now, slowly pacing the room. His eyes stare at the ceiling. "Ah, that is a gift I've possessed a long time. Even when I lived amongst the heavens, even when I walked the Silver Gardens." He pauses, taking a bite of his apple. "I suppose, you would have called me an angel of death. A crude term, but also elegant in its

simplicity. For that, Arianna, is what I am. What I do."
He walks up to me, meeting my gaze. "I deal in death."

He starts pacing again. "You see, my father
bestowed two gifts upon his sons. Each of great power.
To my brother, he gave the ability to take life away. So
easy it is for him. All he needs is but a touch. To me,
my father bestowed the ability to bring life back. All
it takes is a simple caress." He sighs. "There are limi-
tations however. The body must be relatively fresh.
I can regenerate some tissue, but I cannot regrow a
body from ash or a pile of bones. And of course, there
is the greatest limitation of all. I cannot reborn a
vampire."

He sits back down, his head heavy, his eyes dark.
"It is part of the curse you see. When my brother cast us
out and made us vampires, he changed our very being,
changed us, so that my gift could not affect our kind. So
when the time came, I could not save my wife. I could
not save my daughter. In the end, my gift proved near
useless. That is, until I found you."

For a fleeting moment, I feel a tinge of sympathy.
To have power but be unable to use it help the ones you
love…too often have I felt the same. But my compassion
for him fades. This is the man who slaughtered the Fae.
The man who trapped my mother. Despite my hatred, I
decide to continue the current thread of conversation.
For whatever reason, Lucian is sharing, which I haven't

seen him do before. "Why me?" I ask. "What makes me so special?"

He leans closer, his voice soft. "You are the last High Fae. The only one who could summon Yami to this world. And in him lies a power lost to the ages. A power that can change things forever."

I shake my head, puzzled. "And what do you need power for? You already ruled Inferna. You had driven the Fae back. What could you possibly want..." And then it hits me. The pieces fall into place. "You want to go home. You want to return to the Silver Gardens."

He takes a long deep breath and sits taller, as if a weight has lifted. "Finally, someone knows. It's been so hard, you see, keeping this a secret."

"Why keep it a secret at all? Your sons would support you." This I know. Asher has told me of how he dreams of home.

"They would not," says Lucian. "Not if they knew what it entailed. I began to reveal details to Fen and he poisoned me. The others...the others would have done far worse."

"What does it entail?"

He tilts his head. "Come now, you can't expect me to tell you everything."

"The Fae," I spit out, my mind racing. "You need the Fae back in power. You need the Midnight Star to return. You needed..." something that never crossed my mind before, "...you needed the Druids. You needed the Spirits. And then..." *Then...* The idea scratches at my mind, just outside the reach of my conscious mind. *Then...then...then...*

Lucian chuckles. "You do not know yet. That is good. I must leave some surprise, after all."

A thought crosses my mind then. Something I hadn't realized, and I start to shake. "My baby. My baby has vampire blood—"

"Calm now. Your baby is but part vampire. There is more Fae and human there. More than enough to let my gift work. Focus your energies. And you will feel the child within you."

I do as he suggests. Calming my breath. Focusing my mind like Varis taught me. And then I feel it. An energy that is not my own. The energy of my baby. Of Fen's baby.

I miss him then. I miss him so much the pains tears at me like a beast inside my chest trying to escape.

"Come," Lucian says, smacking the side of my bed. "It must have been a while since you've been outside the walls. Let us walk. That is, if you can manage it."

I do not wish to be with him, but the thought of leaving my room does tempt me, and I need to relieve myself something fierce. I push myself to stand, finding I have enough energy to walk. Maybe even run. For the first time, I realize someone must have changed my clothes. I wear a white dress, like I did before, but it is clean, spotless. My last dress would have been stained with red. He comes to mind then. Only now. That is how little he means to me. "What of Levi?" I ask. "Where is he?"

Lucan doesn't skip a beat. "His punishment continues. More severely now, since he tried to escape."

"And Yami? What has happened to my dragon?" I reach for him with my magic, but feel only emptiness, just as before.

"He is still as he was. Unharmed, and secure."

"You mean trapped. Imprisoned. Cut off from me, from our bond."

"If that's how you wish to perceive it, but there are many ways to see the truth, Arianna."

We don't say anymore then, and I use the washroom provided to me and then follow Lucian outside the door and through the grey halls. Somewhere in the distance, men and women shout and laugh. The sounds grow louder as we walk. "What's going on—"

And then I see it. As we turn the corner, I see...

A great hall. Filled with Fae, dark skinned and light, cluttering both sides of the room, between them one open path. And on that path walks Levi.

Naked.

Battered.

His skin covered in red cuts and purple bruises.

People throw food at him. Sticks and stones.

A tomato explodes against his head, staining his silver hair red.

He keeps walking.

A stick hits his legs, causing him to stumble.

He keeps walking.

Someone yells a joke about his genitals.

He keeps walking.

I remember my own walk, the walk Levi put me through. And though I hate the Prince of Envy, I don't think anyone should have to endure such a thing.

To my side, Lucian chuckles.

He chuckles. Like the frenzied mob. And I remember the tale Levi told me. The tale of a disapproving father and a son desperate to honor him.

"Shall we continue?" I ask, gesturing down the hallway.

Lucian pauses. "Yes. Yes, I think I grow bored already. Follow me."

He leads me away from the hall, up a set of stairs, and the yelling and laughing fades. Still, I hear it in my mind. In my memories. Things like that don't leave you. Not truly.

We stop at a great giant door of stone, carved with symbols of beasts. Lucian pushes it open with one hand. We emerge onto a snow-covered mountain, the wind howling around us. Lucian offers me his fur coat.

"No," I say. I'd rather freeze than wear his clothing. But…I remember I must think of the baby. I focus inward, recalling one of the tricks Varis taught me, and my body begins to warm from within. Soon the ice-cold wind feels like a summer breeze.

"Impressive," says Lucian. He must sense the power within me. He continues walking on a path down the mountain. "Have you been here before?"

All the snow. I have not been to a part of Avakiri so cold. I look around for any recognizable landmarks. In the far distance, I see what seems a castle. Grey. Twisted. That is no structure of Fae. It seems…"We're not in Avakiri, are we? We're in Inferna."

He nods.

"Why?"

"There is something here," he says. "Something important to Metsi and me."

Something appears on the horizon. A ruin of ancient stone. Pillars shattered and laying on their side. Archways missing chunks of rock. Statues of men and animals stand tall, some missing a nose, others a hand. The architecture is familiar. It reminds me of the ruins Dean and I uncovered in his realm. The ruins where we found the Mirror of Idis.

Despite my spell, my body starts to cool as we enter the ruin. There is a power here. A force I can feel but not name. "This is why we're here," I say. "You seek something in the ruin."

Lucan raises an eyebrow. "Clever girl. Did you know the Ancient Fae had powers far surpassing those the Fae possess now?"

"I've seen hints."

"It is because the Primal One left them, you know, that they fell into disarray. Without a proper ruler, the Four Tribes grew more and more distant, more and more different. In time, they forgot the power of unity. Each tribe sought more power. They dabbled with things best left untouched. And eventually, it destroyed them."

"The Darkness," I say, growing colder just at the mention of the word.

He nods. "They did not know how to control it. And so it consumed them."

"What of the High Fae? Why didn't they stop it? Prevent the rituals?" But maybe they tried. Maybe they tried like Varis tried to prevent my own ritual, when the Darkness drove Yami mad.

"The High Fae were more advisors than real rulers," says Lucian, waving his hand dismissively. "No one listened to them the way they did the Primal One. It was only after the collapse, after the Ancient Fae died off, that the High Fae tightened their rule to prevent such disasters in the future."

Suddenly, a deep chill seeps into my bones. And despite my magic, I tremble.

"Ah," says Lucian. "We are here."

I follow his gaze to the end of the ruin. There, carved into the mountain, stands a giant grey door, a tree engraved on its center. The wind moves oddly here. Pulsing, beating like a heart. And on the cold air, carries a whisper. A soft caress. It draws me. Pulls me closer to the door. Without thinking, I find myself walking forward. Closer. Closer. With each step, my limbs grow colder, my skin turns paler. Frost builds on my eyelashes, on my hair. But I do not care. I not feel the chill. Not anymore. Instead I feel warmth. The warmth of a soft embrace. When I lay my hand upon the door, a flash of energy courses through my body, like a lover's touch. And when I lay my ear against the stone. I hear it. I feel it.

The Darkness.

8

MARASPHYR

Fenris Vane

*"There is too much temptation to touch her, to hold
her, and having her so close but not quite close enough
is a sweet kind of torture I am unused to."*

—Fenris Vane

We ride for Grey Mountain. Deep into the realm of
Envy. Deep into Levi's territory. Even with him gone,
we must be careful. If the Princes of War and Lust were
spotted traveling to the mountains, word could reach
Metsi, giving her time to escape and take Arianna with
her. This I will not allow.

So we wear illusions and avoid conversation that
would reveal too much. Even Baron is under illusion to
look like a dog rather than a wolf. I thought Dean would
find it a nuisance, but there is a fire in his eyes, a focus.
All thoughts but those of Arianna seem burned from

his mind. "When we arrive," he says, as we travel on an empty road, "leave the Druid to me. Focus on Arianna. Get her out."

I guide my steed to stay on the dirt path between fields of snow. Dean rides to my right, Tavian to my left and Baron runs ahead, sniffing out our path. We are a meager group, but it is best to travel with fewer people. Less noticeable. Asher needed to stay to manage the realms. Varis chose to stay and keep an eye on the increasingly worrisome Asher. And Tavian…he surprised me by insisting on coming. "If I do not help you rescue Arianna, Kayla would never forgive me," he'd said. I think also he needed a task with purpose to take his mind off Kayla's diminishing health.

We rode hard the first day, but our horses needed rest, so now we travel at a slow canter. Until we can make haste once more. "We will need our combined strength to defeat Metsi," I say. "We must—"

"I don't care about beating her," says Dean, glaring at the horizon, at the setting orange sun. "I will distract her. You will save Arianna. If I fall in battle, so be it."

I have never seen such fervor from my brother. He seems consumed. But then again, so am I. My thoughts are of Arianna and nothing else. "Very well. We will do as you say."

Tavian nods in agreement.

We speak little then. Until we near the Crimson Castle.

It stands in the distance upon a hill of snow. Red clay leaks from beneath the earth, staining the white land red. The castle itself is built from pale blue stone, its spires jagged and sharp, its ceilings arched. Stone statues loom above the entry way, cruel beasts stalking those below. There is a darkness to the castle. A feeling that makes your hair stand on end. Arianna would call it gothic, I think. But there is something more, hidden behind the layers of twisted beauty. A cruelty. A meanness you can taste.

I turn away, not wishing to look upon the monstrosity. Around us, buildings sprout out from the snow, wooden shacks belonging to the poor living on the outskirts of the city. Some have roofs already caved in. Others are missing doors.

Tavian watches the Fae who we pass by, the slaves wearing nothing but tattered robes that barely cover their bodies, though the day is cold and harsh. They tremble, warming their hands with their breath, as they rush from one duty to another. An older Fae, his hair long and grey, collapses in the snow. None seem to notice. None stop to help.

I jump down from my horse and rush to his side. I pull off my thick fur cloak and wrap it around the man.

I bring a flask of water to his lips. Baron whimpers and leans into the man to offer him warmth.

His words are barely a whisper. "Thank you, my prince."

Prince? But the illusion..."I...do not know what you mean."

He smiles. "Your secrets are safe with me. I have heard of tales of the Prince of War. What other vampire would treat a Fae with such kindness?" His eyes flicker to Baron. "And travel with such a loyal companion."

I grin, despite myself. I do not know what the Fae expect of me, or if they hope for things I will never bring, but right now, I grin. I grin for the old man before me. That is a kindness I can do.

Tavian leans down beside me. He offers a portion of his food to the old man, and the man eats, slowly, but steadily.

"We must move on," says Dean from atop his horse, though in his eyes, I see he wishes we could stay, wishes we could do more for these people.

But he is right.

We leave the old Fae with a fur cloak, water and food, and we ride for the mountain. Then we smell the death. The decay. Crosses stand on the side of the road, bloody corpses dangling from their beams, their eyes picked out by crows. My stomach twists and sickens at the sight. I try to look away, but they are all around me. They go down the path as far as the eye can see.

"By the Spirits," whispers Tavian, "why would your brother do this?"

"Levi would rather rule with terror than respect," says Dean, his face twisted in a scowl.

I force myself to face the corpses. To remind myself why I fight against Levi. I try to muster up a rage, and yet, in the end, I only feel pity. Pity for the Fae. Pity for Levi. "You assume he has a choice," I say.

Dean frowns. "Everyone has a choice."

"Do they?" I whisper. "We can choose how to act, to be sure, but can we ever know all the consequences? And if we don't know all the consequences, can we ever really choose our fate?"

"You're being awfully philosophical, brother," says Dean. "Should I be worried?"

I chuckle. "Perhaps." The joke seems to lighten our spirits.

Except Tavian. He looks down at the dirt, away from the corpses, his voice soft. "There is truth to what you say, Fenris. One choice has many branching paths. Your brother, Levi, if defeated, will be remembered as a tyrant, a ruler of fear, yes. But what if he wins? What if he becomes king and destroys all Fae? Then those who are left, the vampires, how will they see him? Likely with respect, envy. And so Levi makes one choice, to torture the Fae and yet, in the end, he may be remembered as many different things."

I nod, wondering how I will be remembered. Will I be the king who ruled by Arianna's side? The Prince who threw away the crown? Or the warrior who let the Midnight Star die? Perhaps something else entirely.

My horse stops. Baron growls. Something is wrong. I was distracted by my thoughts. A fatal error.

I look up, pulling myself back to the present.

"This will be a problem," says Tavian.

Dean clenches his jaw. "Bloody hell."

I see what they mean.

A blockade stands on the horizon, wooden palisades, soldiers, all blocking further entry into the realm. Levi's crimson banners hang from the fortifications.

"When did the bastard set this up?" asks Dean, weaving his horse left and right to get a better view.

"Maybe when he took Stonehill," I suggest. "Or perhaps his Generals set it up after he disappeared. Niam is planning to take the realm."

Dean mumbles under his breath. "Stupid Levi. He's a giant pain in the ass even when he's missing."

"Calm brother. We'll find a way."

Tavian moves his horse to my side. "Do we fight our way in?"

I study the blockade, counting the soldiers I see and estimating the ones hiding behind the wall. "No. There are too many. Hundreds by my count. Even if we could defeat them, and I doubt it, the battle would span days."

"We could fly over," says Dean. "That is, Varis could fly us over."

"Too late to backtrack now," I growl, wishing for a better idea. "Every day we waste is a day Arianna is in danger. Varis it too far. But..."

Dean raises an eyebrow. "But what?"

I turn to him slowly, my face melancholy. "There is someone who could help us."

Dean waits in silence for me to fill him in, a quizzical look on his face.

"Must I spell it out for you, brother?" I ask.

He grins. "Apparently. Since I've no notion who you're talking about."

"We could visit *her*."

"Her?" His eyes light up with realization. "Oh, *her*." He starts to laugh like a madman. "Oh, this will be interesting. Tavian, you're going to *love* this."

"What?" asks the Fae. "Who are we visiting?"

"Marasphyr," I grumble reluctantly.

"An old lover of Fen's," explains Dean.

"This sounds..." Tavian pauses. "Complicated." He doesn't seem to find the notion funny. His face is grim.

And I feel the way he looks.

...

It's a short journey away from the road to reach the Grey Forest. It is a place more dead than alive. Filled with pale white trees and withered grass. Insects surface from the damp mud earth, but no other beasts make noise or appearance. Trinkets, spun from twine to look like puppets hang from branches; an old custom to keep beasts within the forest and away from villagers. And there, deep in the wood, between the trees that bend like claws, we find the cottage. Her cottage.

It's small, built of wood and bricks, but elegant in its design. The main door is thick and carved from a deep red oak. The windows are filled with colorful designs. There is a change as we near the home.

The air smells crisper, cleaner.

The grass turns from withered to lush and green.

Orange lights float in the sky. Fireflies, drifting over a garden of purple and white flowers.

"There is power here," says Tavian as we dismount our horses and walk for the door. "Who is this friend of yours? A Fae?"

"Not exactly," I say, stopping at the doorway, hoping we haven't travelled for nothing. And then I knock.

"I'm out back."

The voice carries unnaturally. Close, intimate like a whisper, yet distant all the same. And smooth. Smooth and rich like honey.

Dean breathes the air in deeply, as if savoring a taste. "Oh, I missed her," he says. "Haven't you, Fenris?"

I remind myself of all the reasons we didn't work. Of why we can't work. "I'm here for Arianna. Nothing else."

Dean grins. "Fine by me."

We walk around the cottage, to a backyard filled with fresh grass and flowers. Butterflies and bees hover over the plants and a deer stalks near the trees, unflinching at our presence. At the center of the garden lies a pool of clear blue water, lilies floating on the surface, crystals glowing below. And there swims Marasphyr, the lower half of her body a tail and fins, her scales a glittering sapphire. Her upper body, well, very human, and very naked.

Dean whistles. "Oh, I *did* miss her."

"Focus," I hiss.

"A mermaid?" says Tavian, staring at the pond. He's not entranced like Dean however. No. There is an uneasiness about him. Perhaps he's never met a mermaid before. They're not common. Not on this world anyway.

Marasphyr breaks through the surface, flipping back her long aquamarine hair, and reclining at the edge of the pool. "Right on time, Fenris." She smiles, her teeth bright and perfect. Not sharp like they were before, like they are naturally.

The illusions we wear don't seem to affect her. I'm not surprised. Not with her power.

Tavian raises an eyebrow. "She knew we were coming?"

I sigh. "Marasphyr remembers things..." I sigh again. "From the future."

Tavian tenses. "That...that is no natural gift."

"Who's to say, my dear?" asks the mermaid. "Aren't we all natural beings? Isn't every part of us a thing to be cherished?"

"Some things we should keep at bay," says Tavian, his eyes dark. "Our faults. Our shortcomings. Even our gifts if they do more harm than good." He turns to me and Dean. "We should go. This place, this magic, it is not something to trifle with."

"She's our only chance," I growl, turning back to the mermaid.

"Ah, Fenris, moody as ever, I see. I suppose you're looking for the lost princess? Word gets around."

I step forward, closer to the pool. "There's a blockade. We need to get past it."

"Hmm...give me a moment." Marasphyr waves her hand and the water around her shimmers and swirls, seeping into her tail, slowly turning it to legs. She walks out of the pool, and as she does, clothing begins to weave around her, covering her pale skin. A black and purple dress falls down her body, cut at the sides to reveal her legs and leather boots. Her hair is already dry, her eyes dark and calling. She locks me with her gaze. Traps me. I—

I look away. There is something about Marasphyr. Something that draws men to her. I suppose Dean has the same effect on women. Maybe they *would* make a great pair.

"So, will you help or not?" I ask.

"Oh, to have the mighty Fenris in my debt I would do anything." She walks forward, to my brother, and runs a finger over his chest. The whole time she looks at me. "But first, I must—"

"We have no time to haggle," I say, clenching my fists. "We've wasted too much time already."

She doesn't react. Just keeps her eyes locked on me. "But first...I must speak to your friend here."

"Tavian?"

"Yes, Tavian." Finally, she looks away from me and at the traveler. At the Fae full of secrets. "It will be quick, I promise."

Tavian grinds his teeth. "I suppose it was to happen eventually."

"What do you mean?" I ask, looking between the Fae and the mermaid.

Marasphyr smiles. "Tavian and I know each other. From the past. And we have an unresolved matter."

Dean drops his jaw. "You knew her? Why not tell us?"

Tavian sighs. "She went by a different name then. A different face too. But..." He looks at her. "It is you, isn't it?"

She winks at him, then takes him by the arm. "Come, old friend. Let's not keep the gentlemen waiting." She guides him away, into the cottage.

I want to stop them. Ask questions. But that would only waste time. I need to get to Arianna.

Dean tries to follow the pair, but the door shuts behind them on its own. Doesn't pry open.

"What do you think that was about?" asks my brother.

"I don't care. Marasphyr is...old."

"Doesn't look it."

"You know what I mean. She is ancient. The Fae is too. They had more centuries than us to cross paths. And if we were to try to understand every detail of their past, it would take centuries more of conversation."

Dean nods, rubbing his chin. "Hmm. Never thought about it that way. Every immortal I've cared for I've grown up with. Shared in most parts of their life. Having a relationship with a mermaid *would* be complicated. There would always be secrets. Even if not intentionally, there would always be information omitted, simply because there was too much information. Is that why it didn't work between the two of you?"

"One of the reasons," I say, not wishing to discuss things further.

Dean begins pacing. "But, I'm a forgiving man. A man who likes to live in the present rather than dwell in the past. Do you think Marasphyr and I could—"

"Maybe."

He stops walking. "I could live with maybe."

I chuckle at my brother's antics. I suppose this is his way of moving on from Arianna. His way of trying.

Marasphyr and Tavian emerge from the cottage, him looking tired and beaten, her more chipper than ever. "Matters have been settled," she says. "For now, anyway. Come. We must make haste."

She snaps her fingers and a gust of wind hits me in the chest, almost knocking me over. The air turns cold and still. The grass begins to die. The pool freezes over. At its center, a shadow gathers. It pulses, like a black heart, humming, then explodes out, turning into a whirlpool of darkness.

Dean points at the thing. "Is that a portal?"

I nod. "How else were we getting past the blockade?"

The four of us walk forward. Into the portal.

And onto Grey Mountain.

9

A HOWL ON THE WIND

"It is loud, all consuming, layered like a chorus. It is soft and hard at the same time. It is gentle and furious. Not female or male. Something else. It surrounds me. It embraces and engulfs me."

—Arianna Spero

I do not know how long I stood at the door, feeling the Darkness pulse on the other side. It could have been minutes. Hours. Days. To me it felt an eternity. To me, it felt like being in a dream. A perfect dream from which none wish to wake. Where Fen and I and our baby lived happily in Stonehill. Where my mother ate with us and held her grandchild on her lap. Where we were safe. Peaceful.

And then Lucian pulled me away.

"It's almost time now," he says.

I blink, trying to focus on the present. The dream calls so strongly. "Time...time for what?"

He winks. "For everything to change."

I try to ask for more, but then she arrives.

Her long blue dress flowing behind her. Her silver jewelry swaying from her neck. Her pale serpent coiled around her arm. Metsi.

A wave of water moves in her wake, controlled by her powers. *She's drawing from the snow*, I realize. Creating water from the ice. Something glides inside the waves. A cage.

Yami!

Metsi stops before us, and with a flick of her hand, the water releases the cage, lowering it to the ground before us. Inside, a small Yami curls up into a ball, wet and trembling. But when he sees me, his eyes light up, and he jumps up and down, screeching, his tongue wagging.

I fall to my knees, beaming, reaching for him. My hands touch the cage, and a shock hits me, pushing me back. The wards. The wards that keep Yami trapped keep me from freeing him as well.

"Let him go!" I growl.

Metsi and Lucian ignore me, facing each other. "I brought the others as well," says the Water Druid. "As you requested." She snaps her fingers, and the wave of water dissipates. In its stead, a woman falls to the ground. Her hands bound behind her back. Her hair blue.

"Kayla!" I rush to her, untying her hands, and checking her for wounds. She seems fine. Better than last I saw her. But she is stunned, voiceless, not entirely conscious.

Lucian and Metsi don't stop me. They don't seem to care.

More of the water dissipates, and two more bodies fall to the ground. Asher and Varis. They don't move, and for a second I think they're dead, but then I notice a subtle rising of their chests. Okay. They're only unconscious.

But how is this possible? Did Lucian capture Stonehill?

"Ari..." Kayla looks up, her voice weak and thin. "Ari," she says again, this time stronger, hugging me tightly. "I'm sorry," she says. "I couldn't stop him. I couldn't stop..." And then she notices him over my shoulder. "I couldn't stop Lucian," she says, rage filling her voice. She dashes forward, hands out like claws. Out for blood.

But then water shoots up around her, curls around her arms like shackles, and pulls her back down to the ground.

"Where is he?" Kayla hisses. "Where is Riku?"

Riku? The Spirit?

"Do not worry, girl," says Lucian, pulling a silver stone from his pocket. "Riku is right here. Safe. So is Zyra." He pulls out another stone. A white one.

Tears well in Kayla's eyes. "What have you done to them?"

"Spirits can take on many forms. They often turn into physical objects when they lack power," says Lucian.

He's right. I remember when Yami turned into a necklace on earth.

Lucian continues, " I simply forced Riku and Zyra into a state they cannot leave on their own. A simple trick really, if one knows the way. Now, I believe it's time I did the same for Yami." He draws a black stone from his pocket and holds it to the cage, whispering words under his breath.

Yami starts to howl.

"You bastard!" I roar. I try to lunge forward, but the water grabs me, holds me down like it does Kayla.

Lucian continues to whisper. And as he does Yami begins to dematerialize. His limbs fade. His voice quiets. In time, he becomes a cloud of black smoke, and the smoke pours into the stone. Until there is no Yami left. The stone has changed, I notice. It is no longer simply dark. It glitters like stars and midnight.

"What are you doing?" I ask. "If you've hurt him I will kill you." My threats are empty, hollow, as tears choke my throat. I thought I couldn't feel Yami before, but now I realize that wasn't entirely true. He'd been there, at the edges of my senses, and now I feel his pain, his terror. He's trapped and I can do nothing to free him. I must think. I must figure out how to fix this.

He said he has Zyra…but also Riku? I look up, into his evil eyes, as the pieces of the puzzle scatter before me. "How is Riku here?"

Lucian frowns. "Don't you know? Kayla here is the new Fire Druid. She is Riku's Keeper. And, like you yourself surmised, I need the Spirits. I need the Druids too. For the Spirits to be at full strength both Keeper and Spirit must be close. Capturing Varis was…simple. Especially when he thought I was his lover."

I grimace. "What do you mean?"

"Isn't it obvious?"

"He used illusion," says Kayla, her eyes burning with hate.

Lucian smiles. "Indeed. For near two months I've impersonated Asher. And all the while no one noticed. How tragic."

Metsi groans. "Stop wasting time on the half-bloods," she tells Lucian. "Are they almost here?"

"Yes," says the vampire king. "I have spied them on the road. They are near. I couldn't tell Fen our location; he would have assumed it a trap. But I mentioned Grey Mountain and planted the seed."

Metsi's eyes flicker to the ruins, to the shadows where someone may hide. They flicker to the door. The door where Darkness lives. "Are you sure about this? Oren did not approve. He—"

"Oren is no longer here," yells Lucian. "If we had done the ritual earlier, perhaps he still would be."

Metsi drops her gaze. She fumbles with her fingers. I have never seen her like this. Nervous. "But what if we can't control it?"

"I have spent millennia preparing the for the ritual. It will happen as we plan."

Metsi nods, though still she trembles.

My mind is racing, trying to decipher what they're saying. "The ritual?" I ask. "You wish to summon the Darkness. But what of the Ancient Fae? You said yourself the Darkness could not be controlled."

He swings his hand through the air. Smashes it across my cheek.

I fall back, my face burning.

Lucian looms over me. His words seep with rage, as if I offended him personally. The cold calculations are gone. It is his curse, I think. The curse of wrath.

"I said *they* could not control it," he yells. "Because they were fools. They missed something so simple. Only one ever tamed the Darkness. And he had the Spirits in his power."

"The Primal One," I whisper.

He nods, smiling. "The Primal One. I shall do as he did. But instead of locking the Darkness away, I will bend it to my will. There is no good or bad in the world. No right or wrong. Not truly. There is dark. There is light. And both are needed. Both are required for life. Locking the Darkness away was a mistake. A mistake I intend to rectify."

His eyes flick up then. And his grin widens, as if he knows a secret none else is privy to. "Ah," he says. "They are here."

And then I hear it.

A howl on the wind.

10

GREY MOUNTAIN

Fenris Vane

"You are a dog. And you will know your place at your master's heel."
—King Lucian

Something is wrong. Instincts honed over centuries tell me to retreat. To flee. We are not in control here. Someone has set a trap. But I cannot run. I cannot leave Arianna.

"What's wrong?" asks Dean, grabbing my shoulder. We sit behind a broken pillar, hiding from view, our swords at the ready. Baron lies at my heel.

"It's nothing," I say, refusing to worry my comrades as well.

"We should not be at this place," whispers Tavian. "There is a power here. A power best left undisturbed."

Marasphyr rolls her eyes. "You and your superstations, Tavian."

He glares at her, unsaid words hanging between them.

"This is where we saw the patrols," I say, remembering what we noticed upon arriving at the mountain. "This is where we will find another. Capture him. Force him to take us to Arianna."

"Should not be here," Tavian says again.

I pretend to shrug off his warning, but in truth I agree. There is something about this ruin. A feeling. A presence. I study the grey stones and the Fae statues. They seem to look at me. They seem to be alive.

"There," whispers Tavian. "A patrol."

I glance over the pillar. That is no patrol That is... Arianna!

I jump to my feet. My heart pounding in my chest. My body ready for battle.

Dean pulls me back. "Patience brother," he hisses under his breath. "Do you not see who she is with?"

I look again, clenching my jaw. "Lucian."

"We cannot beat him, brother," says Dean.

"There are four of us."

"You know it doesn't matter."

Marasphyr fidgets with a ring on her finger. "I'm afraid he's right. I do not wish to face the vampire king."

I sigh, falling back against the stone, cursing the day. Metsi I was prepared for, but Lucian...He is the man who killed the last Midnight Star. The man who slaughtered an entire family of High Fae.

I wasn't there when it happened, but the tales still bring dread. Still, they could be exaggerated, could they not? I know better than most how a story could grow into ridiculous fantasy. My time at Grey Mountain taught me that.

"What do you propose we do, then?" I ask. "I am not letting her go. Not again."

Dean pauses for a moment. "We wait. Lucian cannot guard her every moment. I'm sure he has other matters. We wait. Follow them if we must. And when he leaves, we strike."

Every part of my being wishes to refuse. To attack now. Every part but one. Arianna would not wish me to die foolishly. She would wish for me to live. For both of us to live together.

So I wait.

And wait.

Lucian does not leave.

Instead, someone else arrives. Metsi.

From the shadows, I watch them. They talk. And then Metsi dispels a wave of water, revealing a woman on the ground. She looks familiar from a distance. Kayla!

Tavian tenses at my side, raising his blade. "How could she be here?" he growls.

"Easy, now," says Dean. "We cannot fight both Lucian and Metsi. That is even more certain."

"And what if we wait too long?" I say. "What if they change their minds and kill them?"

"Father always has a plan. If that plan involved Ari and Kayla dead, they would be."

"But you know how he can be," I say, looking my brother in the eyes. "You know rage drives him as much as logic."

Dean says nothing.

I look back to Arianna. Two more bodies fall to the ground. Asher and Varis. "How?" I whisper. "Has Stonehill fallen?"

Dean shrugs, fear in his eyes.

There are raised voices now. Then...

Then Lucian smashes Arianna across the face. I feel the blow in my own gut.

He yells at her. His hand falls on his sword.

No! I will not lose her again.

I jump over the pillar, charging forward.

Baron follows at my heel, howling.

Tavian rushes after me, yelling a cry for battle, Marasphyr right behind him.

Dean follows last. But he follows. I notice the fervor in his eyes. In the end, he will do anything for Arianna.

Together, we charge.

It is a mistake.

Lucian turns, looks into my eyes, and smiles.

He knew we were coming. Somehow, he knew.

Or more likely, he planned for it. This is what he wanted all along.

We should turn back. But I cannot. I will not. For Arianna. For our child, if what Dean says is true.

Lucian gestures to Metsi, and she pulls a purple vial from her robes. She holds it up with one hand, then shatters it in her grip. The purple liquid spills out and starts to morph, changing into mist. She's using her powers. Turning whatever that concoction is airborne.

And then, she pushes it our way.

"Hold your breath!" I yell, but I'm too late.

The purple mist hits us like a gust of wind, seeping into our lungs. It tastes bitter at first, and then, it doesn't taste at all, turning my mouth numb. Then my chest, then my arms, then my legs.

I collapse, my sword falling from my paralyzed hand.

The others, Dean, Tavian, Marasphyr, and even Baron fall too. I turn my head a little to see them. It seems the only part of my body not fully paralyzed.

"Fen!" yells Arianna, restrained by shackles made of water, her eyes full of tears. Happy or sad I cannot tell. She glares at Lucian. "Let them go!"

Lucian laughs, looking at me. "The Purple Sleep. A rare concoction, but worth it for this occasion. Don't worry. You will regain mobility and feeling soon." He paces between our frozen bodies, stopping at Baron. Then he pulls out a small grey stone and whispers incantations under his breath.

Baron's head flinches with pain. He howls, as if something is eating him from within. He writhes on the ground and I can do nothing to help him. I feel his pain and panic in my own body, and it consumes me. Then he begins to fade, turning into smoke.

I try to cry out. To fight for my friend. But not even my lips move.

Lucian seems to notice my struggle. "Do not fear, Fenris. Tauren—that is, Baron—will be fine. Everything will be fine."

The spell ends, and Baron disappears into the stone. What is the meaning of this? Why does he need my Spirit?

Lucian turns to Metsi. "See, everything is as I planned. Now, for the final Spirit…"

She clenches her jaw, shaking, then slowly lifts up her arm with Wadu. "We'll be together again soon," she whispers to her Spirit.

Then Lucian pulls out another stone, a blue one, and mutters the incantations again. Wadu screeches and hisses, while Metsi's eyes swell with tears. "I'm sorry. But this is for the best. For us all." The screeching fades, and Wadu disappears into the stone.

Lucian pockets the Spirit and walks down the ruins, to the stone door carved into the mountain.

Someone mumbles something. Asher. He's starting to wake. Varis too. I see their fingers twitch.

"Behold," says Lucian, drawing all five stones. "The power of the Primal One in the palm of my hand. Wadu, Riku, Tauren, Zyra, and Yami. Water, fire, earth, wind, and the Midnight Star." He gestures to the middle of the door. There is something in the center. A hand print. It reminds me of the Waystones. It must be the lock. Lucian murmurs something, and all five stones float into the air. Then they shoot across the sky, embedding themselves into the stone, making a perfect circle around the handprint. Each stone, each Spirit, starts to glow. A rainbow of colors.

Arianna sits up taller. "Don't do this, Lucian. You cannot control the Darkness. No one can."

The vampire king looks down, his blue eyes cold. "I will no longer be bound by my brother's curse. First, I take this realm. And then I march on the heavens." He turns to the door and places his hand on the lock.

The earth groans.

The wind trembles.

The sun darkens.

"It comes," whispers Tavian, his eyes rolled back, talking though he was paralyzed. "An unnatural beast. An unseemly creature. The Darkness. The Darkness comes."

A pain erupts inside me, like something bit down on my heart and chewed. Despite the paralysis my body starts to shake, spasm. My limbs stretch out, as if they're trying to tear away in different directions. Some part of me is not my own. Some part wants to leave.

Arianna groans, falling over. Kayla follows. They must feel it too.

Asher seems unaffected, but Varis...

Varis screams in agony, his limbs twisting unnaturally, his eyes rolling back. Metsi does the same. Perhaps because they are full Fae. It seems to affect them the most.

Lightning strikes the sky.

Thunder tears the air.

And rain begins to fall.

For a moment, everything goes quiet. The screaming fades. The wind stills. Even drops of water seem far away.

And then a low growl takes their place. A sound unnatural. A sound that chills to the very core.

The stone door cracks, and with a great moan it erupts open. The five stones swirl through the air, landing on Lucian's arm, twisting around his bracer like a bracelet.

Inside the ancient door, one can see nothing but a pit of black. But it is not empty, no. Something stirs within. When it steps forward, the earth trembles in its wake. When it breathes, the very air turns to ice. And when it roars, the mind wishes for death.

The creature emerges. As tall as a giant oak. As long as a great hall. It walks on all fours, its back legs like hooves, its front like claws. Thick hair covers its body, black and slimy and writhing like snakes. Its face twists and turns, half man, half beast. Its teeth are many, too many, some dull molars, others sharp, long fangs. On its chest, white bone pierces black skin, parts of its ribcage sticking out from its body. This beast is torture to see, and yet, something draws my gaze. Something pulls me closer.

Wisps of black smoke fall from the creature, some of them swirling around Lucian. The smoke becomes viscous, like ink, hanging heavily in the air. Lucian breathes in deeply the vile Darkness, and his veins pulse dark under pale skin, his eyes blacken into orbs of midnight. Then the blackness within him fades, returning to him a normal pallor, his eyes the same cold blue as always, and he smiles. "Finally, we are bound. I feel your power."

The creature talks, whispering in a thousand voices, layered upon each other likes echoes of the dead, cold and lifeless. "What...is your desire?"

"First, we will secure this world. And then we will retake my homeland."

Asher sits up, finally awake. "What have you done, father?"

Lucian grins. "As I said I would, my son. I have brought peace between Fae and vampire. Come. I will show you."

He waves his hand into the air, and a pool of darkness swirls above us. A portal. Like the one Marasphyr can make, but larger, far larger. It grows and grows, until it consumes us all.

For a moment, all I see is shadow.

And then I am on a stone floor, on a plaza. Hundreds of bodies mill around us. I know this place. These people. These buildings. We are at Stonehill!

"Secure the castle," says Lucian to the Darkness.

And chaos follows.

The creature leaps into the air, as high as a mountain, and lands on my castle, where the wall is still broken open. Screams erupt from within.

Around us, people yell and run. But not all. Not even half. Some stay perfectly still, their eyes white, glazed over. The Fae. The Fae do not move.

I look to Varis, to Metsi. They are the same, standing still, faces void of expression or emotion.

"What have you done to them?" Arianna's voice is loud, guttural, angry and terrified.

Asher shakes the Wind Druid, pleading. "Snap out of it. Snap out of it Varis."

Lucian laughs. "He cannot. Do you not understand, I wield the power of the Primal One."

"He..." whispers Arianna, her face sapped of color, her eyes wide in horror. "He controls the Fae. Just like the Primal One did, he controls their will."

I feel the paralysis wearing off, prickling sensation returning to limbs that slept. I push myself up to sit, willing strength back into my body, and look at Tavian. He looks back, his eyes grave, but still his. Somehow, he is not affected. Nor am I, Kayla, or Arianna. It seems only full Fae have lost their will. That must be what I felt when my body was tearing itself apart. It must have been fighting for control. Still, it does not explain Tavian.

"How did Metsi ever agree to this?" asks Kayla.

"She did not," says Lucian. "Not entirely. She knew we were summoning the Darkness. But, she never considered that I would attain power over all Fae. She thought we would destroy the vampires together. Destroy my own people? What a fool she was."

Some of my subjects, the vampires and Shade, rush for the castle, to defend it from the creature. But then Lucian tilts his head, and Varis jumps into the sky. An unnatural wind hits my soldiers, and they fall to the ground, pinned. Those too far to be affected are attacked by their very own slaves, overwhelmed and forced to submit. Metsi conjures water from the snow and waterfalls, sending a tidal wave towards the wall. It hits the guards manning their stations, knocking them out or drowning them.

"You monster," I roar, watching my people decimated and unable to stop it.

"No," says Lucian. "I simply bring peace. The vampires and Shade who surrender, who pledge their allegiance to me, will be left unharmed. And let me be clear…all vampires and Shade."

All. He means us as well. He wants us to swear fealty.

Lucian starts pacing, untouched by the chaos around him. He walks up to Asher. "Let us start with you, my son. I told you everything would be made clear. I told you you'd be freed. Join with me, and together we will conjure a portal to the heavens, and retake the Silver Gardens. Isn't that what you always wanted?"

Asher drops his head, anger and sadness clear upon his face. Then he looks up and spits at his father. "You turned my friends, my lover, into mindless slaves!"

Lucian sighs, as if he expected this. "Yes. I had to. To end your petty war. And to secure an army for the war to come. The war against my brother. So yes, I made them slaves, like the Primal One, but just like the Primal One, I can give them their will back. If you serve by my side, if you help me retake the heavens, I swear to you, Varis will have his will again."

At this, Asher pauses. His breath catches. "I…I…"

"And if you do not side with me," Lucian continues. "Then I will command Varis to slit his own throat right now as you watch. When he dies, some other Fae will inherit his powers, and you will have learned your lesson."

"I..."

"Hmm. You hesitate." Lucian looks to the sky, at Varis, and the Druid raises a dagger, places it against his own throat. "Let's see. On the count of three. One. Two. Thr—"

"Stop!" Asher yells falling forward, clutching his father's boots, crying onto the stone. "I will serve you. I will be by your side. Just keep him alive. Keep him alive!"

Lucian grins, kneeling down and taking his son's hands in his own. "Very well, my son. It will be as you ask."

I can barely watch this sick manipulation. I need to do something to stop this. Slowly, I flex and unflex my hand, testing my mobility. Most of it has returned. My sword is near, teleported along with us.

"And now, my other son, Fenris," says Lucian walking up to me. "Join me and your sister, Kayla, lives. Do not, and I kill her now, transferring her powers to some full Fae who will prove much more useful and submissive."

Kayla shakes her head. "Don't do it, Fen. I don't care if I live."

"Shut up!" roars Lucian. "You care not for your life, but he does. And of course, there is Arianna. I will keep her alive until her baby is born, but how will she live? In comfort or torture? Will she sleep on a soft bed, or on a rack, her body cut into? She can even die, you know, from the pain. I'll just bring her and the baby back. I've done so once already, while you searched for her. Imagine me doing it every day. Imagine her dying over-night, just to reawaken and die again. Can you accept that, Fenris? Can you doom her to such a fate?"

The images his words conjure tear at my heart. I know what Arianna will say. She will say let him torture her. Don't submit. But how can I throw this fate upon her? Upon my child?

I bow my head. "Father, I…"

Then I grab my sword and ram it into Lucian's heart.

He stumbles back, face dumfounded. "I…I did not expect this." He looks at his body oddly, then grabs my blade by the handle and pulls it out. Dark blood covers the steel. He doesn't even seem fazed. How…

"I'm afraid," says Lucian. "It will take more than simple steel to kill me now."

"Steel cannot cut shadow," whispers Tavian.

Lucian nods. "So, what will it be, Fenris? Will you pledge yourself to me, or see Arianna die over and over?"

"I…"

I see something pass between Tavian and Marasphyr. A look. An understanding.

Then the traveler jumps to his feet and dashes forward, his hands extending into claws, turning black. He slashes out for the king.

Lucian steps to the side with ease but...

Two dark portals appear in a blink. One in front of Lucian. One to his side. Conjured by Marasphyr.

Tavian flies into the one before him, jumping out of the one beside Lucian, right where the king stepped, and Tavian strikes.

He does not aim to wound though.

He aims for the stones on Lucian's bracer.

With one blow, his claws rake through Lucian's arm. He hits the stones.

And they shatter.

Orbs of light explode into the air and Lucian falls back, trembling.

The lights whip around, diverging. One heads to me. One to Kayla. One to Arianna.

"Run!" yells Marasphyr. She throws up a hand and another portal opens between us.

I wish to stay, to fight, but if Lucian can't be killed—

"Run!" yells Marasphyr again.

And finally, I move. We all do. Marasphyr, Tavian, and Dean. Even Arianna and Kayla. Shattering the stones must have weakened their bonds. We all jump into the portal.

All except Asher. He stays, weeping. He stays for Varis.

11

MOONLIGHT

"I am the Prince of War. I am the Prince of Death."
—Fenris Vane

Pressure builds around me, as if I'm squeezing through a small opening, but I don't feel any solid walls. Something clutches to my shoulder, and in the darkness, I see...

Yami!

I nudge his little head with my own, and my baby dragon purrs. In the distance, I hear a growl. Baron! When the stones broke, the Spirits must have been freed. They—

The pressure ends, and I tumble onto ground, onto fresh grass. This new place is bright, but I can't tell where the light comes from. I see no sun, no source for the ever-present glow that surrounds me. The grass I'm sitting on is the color of eggplant, and wild flowers grow in clusters around me in every color imaginable. Yami hops off my shoulder to sniff at the flowers, making little squeaking noises of excitement.

The dread I felt at what I just witnessed is temporarily replaced by the joy I feel at having Yami back. I can feel our magic connecting and coiling around each other.

"Arianna?" I hear Fen's voice before I see him. He appears from behind a large tree, his eyes frantic until he sees me. I stand and he runs over to embrace me. "Are you injured?"

My hand falls to my stomach by reflex, to the baby the size of a pea inside me. "No, I'm fine. *We're* fine." I still don't know how Fen feels about the baby. I'm not sure he even knew about the child until Lucian brought it up. What if he doesn't want the baby? What if he...

Fen grabs my hands tenderly in his own. Then he falls to his knees and rests his head on my belly. His voice is heavy. "I feared I'd never see you again. That I would never even meet our child. I..." His voice breaks, cracks with sorrow. "I...I love you, Arianna Spero. I love you."

His words break me. More than anything ever could, his words undo all the composure I'd fought so hard to maintain. I didn't even know how much I needed to hear him say that until he did. He stands and caresses my face in his strong hands, presses his lips against my own, filling me with his taste, his scent of pine and earth. We kiss so fiercely it almost hurts. His hands drop down my back and without warning he scoops me into his arms, cradling me close to his chest. I wrap my arms around his back, running my fingers over his coiled muscle. Pulling at his hair.

It's been too long. Too long since I felt his arms around me. Too long since I tasted his mouth. Too long since I could hold him and feel the heat of his body. So much has happened. So much torture and pain and war. But in the end there is still this. Him. Me. Us.

Near us, Yami and Baron dance and play, chasing each other and running wild through the trees.

"Fen, the others," I pause, pulling my mind away from him for just a moment. Trying to remember why we're here. What we need to do, which is harder than I'd like to admit with the Prince of War looking at me with those sultry blue eyes. "We should look for them. We need to—"

"I don't care," he growls, carrying me forward, past thick trees that cover the sky. He spots a cave, and takes us inside, laying me down on the soft earth, leaving Yami and Baron outside to play and frolic together.

I don't know where we are, or even how safe we are, but everything feels...different. More relaxed. Less urgent. I feel the uncoiling of something in my gut, something that hasn't relaxed in...I don't even know how long.

And in this moment, all I care about is Fen. All I want is Fen. All I need is Fen. Nothing else matters. All my questions, all my worries, the weight of all my future choices, all of that fades into the background. I'll think on it later, I promise myself. Right now, I deserve a moment. We both do.

"Hmm, this seems familiar," I say, grinning. "Reminds me of when I had to heal you."

"I would have healed by myself."

"Right…you were pretty out of it. I wonder, do you remember what happened next?" I ask, biting my lip.

He brushes my cheek with his hand. "We kissed."

"And is kissing all we're going to do this time as well?"

He grabs me and pulls me closer against his hard body, his breath on my ear. "I intend to be more thorough this time, believe me. And I warn you, I will not be delicate." He nibbles at my neck, digging teeth into flesh just enough to sting without breaking skin, and I moan in desire.

Then he turns that bite into a kiss, his mouth running my neck, to my shoulder, then my chest and stomach…then my legs, leaving a trail of heat and desire with every brush of his lips.

I lose myself in ecstasy.

My body trembles without my permission, my fingers digging into the earth. My mouth moves without thought, summoning sounds of pleasure. This is beyond anything I have felt. Anything I imagined.

"Perhaps we should stop," he teases, smiling. "After all, you said the others will—

"Just shut up," I whisper, my breath rabid.

He resumes his methods, gliding his fingers over my body in ways I cannot even comprehend, as if he touches all of me at once. My lips. My breasts. My thighs.

I lose myself to him.

And then we become one. Consumed with desire. Hungry for each other. We do things I never thought I would or could, but I trust him completely, and he me, and so we give everything to each other. I do not know how long we spend in the cave, but after, I can barely stand, and I grin like a fool, basking in the afterglow of something more magical than I've ever felt.

"That was..." I'm at a loss for words. I roll onto my side and glide a finger over his chest.

He grins at me through heavy eyelids. "Our first time together.... It was...influenced by drink. I wasn't at my best."

There's something in his words that make me think he's holding back, but it doesn't matter, because right now everything is as it should be. "Well, if this was your best, I definitely want more."

He kisses me, smiling against my lips. "And I want to give it all to you, Arianna."

Unfortunately, those hassling thoughts, the ticking of time and consequence stir in me, though not as heavily as before. Still..."We should dress. Find the others. They must be worried."

I don't think he hears me at first; he is so still and his expression so distant. I've never seen Fen so relaxed before. It's...disconcerting. But his face shifts and it's as if my words finally land on him. "Yes, you're right. Of course."

He seems off. Confused, but we both dress quickly and leave the cave, albeit reluctantly. My body feels the effects of our lovemaking. I want nothing more than to curl up with him and spend hours in his arms. The pull is strong, but that will have to wait. We've had our moment. Now we must prepare.

Once we leave the cave, Yami and Baron join us, Yami riding on Baron's back and clearly enjoying every moment of it. Baron runs to me and rubs his nose into my hand. I drop to my knee and nuzzle him. "I've missed you too, boy. Thanks for taking care of Fen for me."

Baron gives a quick bark of agreement and I laugh. It feels good to laugh. To smile. To feel pleasure. All the things I'd forgotten how to feel for so long.

"Where should we begin looking?" I ask Fen, as my eyes take in the newness and wonder of this world. "And where are we?"

Fen shrugs. "I've no idea where we are. Marasphyr could have portaled us anywhere. As for where we should begin looking, I think our search is already over." He points ahead and I see a group walking towards us.

Dean, in his black chainmail, Kayla in a green gown—with a phoenix on her shoulder, and the man I saw briefly in the dungeons. He wears a white fur cloak and jewelry made of bone hangs from his neck. And then there's the woman I don't know. The one with long black hair and pale skin. Her marvelous black dress cut down the side to reveal her long legs.

When they get closer, Kayla runs up to us and hugs us both. "Ari, I've been so worried about you."

There's something different about the beautiful Fae who was amongst the first friends I made in Inferna, and one of the best. She looks...aged. Tired. Not her skin or body, but her eyes. "Are *you* ok?" I ask, my tone soft and full of worry.

Something flashes in her eyes and she and the man in the white fur share a look. "I'll be well enough, in time."

She smiles again and holds out her hand to the man. "This is Tavian Gray, a...good friend. Tavian, this is Ari."

Tavian bows his head in a sign of respect. "It is an honor to meet the Midnight Star," he says in a deep voice.

I look between the two of them and smile, then wink at Kayla, who actually blushes. There's definitely more than friend vibes happening here. "It's an honor to meet you as well." I look back to Kayla. "We clearly have to catch up soon," I say with a teasing smile.

Her phoenix chirps and my blood freezes. The last time I saw Riku he was with the fire Druid who tortured me. I still wear the scars, both on my body and in my soul. A moment of panic clutches at my chest and I struggle to breathe. Kayla frowns. "What's wrong?"

Her cool hand touches my arm and I take a deep breath. "I just...I'm shocked you're the new fire Druid."

She looks at Riku with affection, the way I look at Yami. "Not as shocked as I am. We do indeed have much to catch up on."

Dean approaches next, his face a mask. I can't sense what emotions he's holding in, but I remember his declarations to me, and my heart hurts for him. Even still, it's good to see the nearly always shirtless vampire.

"You're actually fully clothed for this occasion," I say, trying to lighten the mood around us.

"It's a temporary set-back, I assure you."

I hug him and he holds me a beat longer, before letting go. When I look to Fen, I expect to see jealousy, but I see only sadness. What have these two been up to, I wonder?

The last one left is the mystery woman looking absolutely stunning and perfectly poised. "Who are you exactly?" I ask, fumbling with my simple white gown.

She raises a perfectly manicured eyebrow. "Don't recognize me?

Fen clears his throat. "This is Marasphyr. The—"

"The mermaid? But your fins? Your teeth?"

"I wanted a different look," she says, shrugging. "Not a difficult thing to change for me."

"But, now you look...you look..." I can't bring myself to say it. Because she looks bloody damn perfect. And Fen had a thing with her.

Before, with the sharp teeth and scales and slimy fins, I wasn't really worried, but now...I guess that answers my question about how you have a fling with a mermaid. They grow legs. And...other parts, presumably.

Fen sighs, wrapping his arm around me, pulling me closer. "Marasphyr helped us rescue you. In exchange for a possible favor from me in the future."

A favor? Oh God. What favor? What if she wants him to—

"There is nothing between us," says Fen, caressing my hands. "Nothing at all." He looks sincere. Honest.

For a second, Marasphyr loses her composure and scowls, but then, just like that, it returns: her perfect smile.

God, I just want to punch those teeth. I…

Okay, Arianna. Okay. Relax. Focus on something else.

"What is this place?" I ask, looking around. "Doesn't look like any of the Seven Realms I've visited."

"Because it's not," says Marasphyr, leaning against a tree. "You might call it a different world entirely, but it's not that either. Not truly. This is a place between worlds. A Rift, if you will. Normal rules don't apply here."

Kayla raises an eyebrow. "Normal rules?"

Tavian puts his arm around her, and they share a look of comfort. "Time moves differently here," he says. "Here, a year is like a week in Inferna. A day is less than a moment."

"Wait," I say, concerns rummaging in my head. "What of my contract? I must spend a month with each prince, and Levi isn't here. Even if he was, my time with him was pretty much over. I was due for another prince."

Fen clenches his fist. "Marasphyr, is her contract in danger of being violated?"

She rolls her eyes. "Relax, Fenris. By the time we leave this place, less than a day will have passed on Inferna. She's allowed to spend a little time away from a prince, isn't she?"

"Correct," says Fen.

"Then everything's fine. When we return, it will be as if we hadn't left. Well, mostly. We will keep our memories of this place, of course."

I wipe my forehead, relieved that my mother will be safe. My mother. All of this was for her, and yet she seems so far away now. I'm nothing like that girl I was when Asher first entered The Roxy. It seems so long ago. Now, my mother isn't the only consideration. Now there are so many other moving pieces to my life, so many people affected by the choices I make. Even thinking of it all makes my head spin, and just as I'm about to say something, the thoughts, the worries, they float away, like magic bubbles. It's all going to work out. I needn't fret. "So, is that why you brought us here?"

Marasphyr waves her hand dismissively. "Not really. Mostly, I took us somewhere Lucian cannot follow. At least, until he learns how, and I don't believe he will. And of course, we have time here. Time to think. To plan. When we return to Inferna, every second will count." She sits down and starts drawing swirls in the earth with her finger.

"And you're helping us—why exactly?" I ask, not wanting Fen to accrue more debts to this woman.

She smiles. "Believe it or not, Inferna is my home. My main home."

"But...I haven't seen any mermaids on Inferna or Avakiri. Aren't you from a different world?"

She looks down, her eyes dark. "I think we have better things to discuss than my past, girl. Like how we defeat the Darkness."

Dean whistles. "Doesn't seem easy, that. I mean, Fen stabbed good old daddy in the chest, and he didn't flinch. And that creature, you know, the ugly one, is it hard to kill too?"

Tavian nods. "Only moonlight steel can harm it."

He seems to know a lot, this Fae. I wonder who is. He doesn't seem that old, with his brown hair. But his eyes speak of a deep wisdom. And he alone was the only Fae not mind-wiped by Lucian's Primal One magic.

Fen frowns. "Moonlight steel? I've never heard of such a thing."

"I have," says Dean, his face lighting up. "It was an artifact of the Ancient Fae, much like the Mirror of Idis. But, I could never find much information on it. They say it was used by the Primal One to fight the Darkness. And, well, of course there was the prince."

"What prince?" asks Fen.

"The Moonlight Prince. Don't you remember?" Dean studies his brother quizzically, then shrugs. "Rumor said the prince had a moonlight sword. Supposedly, it's how he got his nickname."

"It's true," says Tavian.

"Ah, so you worked with the prince, didn't you?" Dean beams. "I knew you were hiding something. You helped him during the rebellion, didn't you?"

Tavian says nothing.

"What rebellion?" asks Fen.

"Really don't remember?" asks Dean. "The Fae had a large uprising long ago, led by someone called the Moonlight Prince. It was sometime, well, I believe sometime after you became a prince."

Fen shakes his head.

Tavian looks grim.

A tension grows in the air.

I butt in before things get crazy. "So, this moonlight steel, how do we get some?"

"Well, the easiest way would be to find the sword," says Tavian. "But..."

"But what?"

"But after the Moonlight Prince vanished, the sword disappeared. Many Fae have searched for it, myself included, and none found the blade."

Marasphyr sighs. "Perhaps we could succeed where you failed."

Tavian scowls at her. "The blade is impossible to find. Trust me. For thousands of years I have wandered, searching for the sword on my path. It is gone."

"Well, it can't be gone," says Marasphyr. "It must be somewhere."

"Yes." The Fae grits his teeth. "Technically, it *is* somewhere, on Inferna or Avakiri most likely. But last I checked, we don't have an extra thousand years to look for it."

Marasphyr shrugs as if to say fine.

"So," I say. "What if we forget the sword? What if we just find some steel?"

Marasphyr laughs. "It would be extremely hard to attain, and even if you did, you need a master smith to forge it into a weapon."

Everyone's eyes dart to Kayla. "We have a master," I say.

"I can forge anything." Kayla places her hands on her hips. "Anything."

"Fine. Fine," says Marasphyr. "But you still need to get the moonlight steel, and you won't."

Now I place my hands on my hips. "Why not?"

"Only someone *worthy* can receive a chunk of moonlight steel. And by worthy, I don't mean they're some cocky hero, or an innocent looking princess. I mean someone unconstrained by flaws, unhindered by doubt. Someone, and I hate to admit it, better than I. And certainly, much better than all of you."

I like this Marasphyr less and less. What did Fen ever see in her?

"But..." Marasphyr drops her eyes. "There is no harm in trying. Perhaps one of you will surprise us all."

"Okay," says Kayla, "but after we get the steel and make the sword, then what? Lucian has an entire race of Fae under his control. Two Druids under his power. And the vampires too scared or dead to oppose him."

"And..." adds Dean. "Let's not forget my lovely brothers. I bet as we speak they're sucking up to good old dad. Levi for sure. He's always looking to please father. Niam without a doubt. He follows power and right now Lucian reeks of it. Asher's under his thumb to save his lover. And Ace...actually, I'm not sure about Ace. But come on, will he really oppose an army of mindless Fae, Lucian, the ugly creature thing, and most of his brothers? That's suicide, and he's no fool."

"What about Zeb?" I ask, remembering the kind prince who treated Fen and I to food in his kingdom.

Dean rubs his chin. "Zeb...I don't think he wants to pledge allegiance. But just like Ace, what choice does he have? He's probably kissing daddy's boots right now."

"You forget," says Marasphyr. "Time moves differently here. When we leave, likely some of your brothers will still not have sworn to Lucian."

"Then we can join forces with them," I say, ideas forming in my mind. "And they must have armies. Vampires and Shade who remain loyal to them."

Dean sighs. "If the Fae haven't overtaken them. Remember, every single slave and servant on Inferna is now under Lucian's control. The Outland raiders are under his control. The men and women in Avakiri. His army spans the entire world."

"But," says Fen, his eyes shifting quickly as he thinks. "If any kingdoms can survive this invasion, it would be the realms of Sloth and Gluttony. Consider their situations. Sloth, due to all of Ace's inventions, has the lowest slave population of all realms. Low enough that the vampires and Shade will easily hold the upper hand. And gluttony: Zeb has a high slave population indeed, but most of them are on water, rowing boats. Most of the vampires and Shade are on land. If the Fae decided to invade from the sea, Zeb can lock his gate, strengthen his defenses, even set the ships on fire from a distance with archers."

I nod. "So there may be two free realms when we return."

Fen tightens his grip on me. "Exactly. Two realms and two armies."

"Using the armies, we draw Lucian out, and kill him with the moonlight blade." I frown. "But we'd have to fight and kill Fae. Fae who are under Lucian's spell and not in control of their choices. That feels... wrong."

Dean shrugs. "It's that or they stay mental prisoners for all eternity. This really is the only way to freedom."

Fen closes his eyes, his voice tired. "Freedom...Oh, this is not the way to freedom."

"What do you mean?" I ask.

He chuckles, then steps away from the group, leaning against a tree and looking out into the distance.

I follow him, even as the others continue to discuss plans. I stand by Fen's side, leaning against his shoulder. "What's wrong?"

He wraps a strong arm around me and I lean into it as he talks. "The way I see it, there are two paths we can take. We can acquire the moonlight steel, forge the sword, return to Inferna and defeat Lucian. Then I can perform the blood ritual, turning you vampire and completing your contract. We'll have an heir, and together you and I will rule the seven realms." His tone harshens. "We'll have to keep peace between Fae and vampire, settle disputes between my brothers, listen to the pleas of every citizen waiting to ask us for one favor or another. At times, we'll disagree on what to do, and as time goes on, we'll disagree more. Eventually, maybe thousands of years from now, we'll forget why we married in the first place. You'll forget why you chose me. And then we'll quarrel. Maybe even fight. Perhaps we'll start a whole new war. Or..." He pauses, his face softening. "We just leave. Right now. We leave the seven realms be, return to earth, and live our life. You, me, and our child. No responsibilities we do not desire. No duties we don't wish to attend."

I grimace. "Life rarely works that way."

"But it can." He takes my hands in his own, caressing them. "We can start that life, a new life of happiness and kindness, together. We can start it now."

"But…what of Asher and Varis?"

"When Asher helps his father reconquer the heavens, Varis will be free. Why should we interfere? I don't care for the angels who cursed thousands of their own, turned them into vampires and sent them to another world to massacre the Fae."

I understand his point. The angels don't seem worth saving. "What of your other brothers? Zeb and Ace."

He shrugs. "They have the same option as us. They can leave their realms right now, live a life of peace. Or they can stay and fight to control their own lands. The choice is up to them. Why should they not face the consequences?"

A part of me can't believe what I'm hearing. The Prince of War speaking of surrender. But a part of me can't help but be swayed by his arguments. For over four months I have been a prisoner of Inferna. Tortured, forced to do terrible deeds to survive. I do not wish to return to such a world. I don't, but…I have a reason. The reason that started it all.

"My mother," I whisper. "I can't leave my mother."

"You won't have to."

My heart stops. "What?"

"We can still fulfill the contract, if you wish. I can turn you, make you vampire. Your mother will be free. And then together, we leave Inferna and Avakiri and all the sorrow they bring."

"I..." I never considered I could free my mother and not actually rule. I'd be a Queen, yes, but only in title. "I...I don't know."

Fen sighs, then breathes in deeply, his eyes full of compassion. "I know what you feel. Even as I say these words, a part of me wishes to rush back to Inferna, to defeat Lucian and reclaim Stonehill. For I am the Prince of War, the Prince of Death. I do not surrender. I do not lose. But, I think...I think I am tired of being a prince. I think I am tired of fighting." He lets go of my hands and sits down, his back against the tree. "For so long I have fought, but it is only recently, since I met you, that I have thought about *why* I fight. For the vampires? They enslaved half a race, killed thousands and have no intention of stopping. The Fae? They captured you, manipulated you to their own ends, seeking to kill every vampire, to wipe away an entire people. And not just them, but the Shade too, because their blood is impure. So, why did I fight? It is only now, I realize, I fought for myself. Because I enjoyed it. The thrill of battle, the ecstasy of victory. Seeing others envious at my abilities. But...I don't care for such things now. At least, I do not wish to. So, let us put an end to fighting. Not by going back and fighting more, but by leaving our swords behind."

He goes down on one knee, taking my hand in his. "Please, Arianna, come with me. Come with me, and

I promise I will do everything I can to bring you happiness every single day of your life. Even if that life is forever."

My eyes fill with tears. My knees feel weak. This is...this is all I wanted. All I could have hoped for. To be with the man I love, raising our child together, my mother alive and free. I want to go with him. I need to. I feel that same vague muting of urgency that I felt in the cave. That same whim to abandon all to my desire for this man. It's hard to fight that. Hard to stay focused on something that doesn't feel nearly as good as giving in.

And yet, I can't.

Because something inside me knows it is the wrong choice. Something inside me pulls be back to Inferna. And it isn't because I enjoy battles or winning. It is because I hope. I hope for a better world. For everyone. And I will never stop.

Dum Spiro Spero.

While I breathe, I hope.

"I'm sorry," I say, pulling back, letting go of his hands as tears sting my eyes. "I'm sorry, but I can't go with you. I need to free the Fae. I need to end the slavery. Because, if I don't, I won't ever be happy, not truly, and that won't be fair to you. It won't be fair to me. And I won't live like that. I'm sorry." Before he can protest more, I turn and run. Run into the forest, tears falling from my eyes.

Behind me, I hear something smash. A fist meeting wood.

I'm sorry. I'm sorry. I'm sorry.

...

I run out of breath by a pond. The waters shimmer with pale blues and greens, and glowing fish swim underneath. Trees sway overhead, though I feel no wind. The air smells of jasmine and roses and honey, though I see none of those things around me. I find a large stone to sit on and ponder my options. I need to go back to Inferna, but what if that means things between Fen and I will never be the same? Can I really choose the Fae over him? When for the first time in his so very long existence he has the chance for peace?

Someone walks up behind me. "What was that all about?" asks Dean. He sits next to me, throwing his arm over my shoulders.

I sigh, trying to relax. "Fen and I...we disagree on what to do next."

"Let me guess, he just wants to say screw it to Inferna and run off with you."

"How do you—"

"Because I'd do the same." He smiles mischievously. "But I can't. So, I will go back to reclaim my

144

realm, to preserve the arts and culture of Inferna and Avakiri."

"Noble goals," I say, resting my chin on my palm.

"More selfish really. I can't live without beauty."

"It's strange, but somehow, going back to fight for the Fae, somehow it feels selfish. Because I'm doing what I want despite what Fen wants. Because in doing so, if I fail, if I die, my mother would forever be trapped by the contract. So…that make any sense?"

He raises an eyebrow. "Well, it's definitely messed up. You want to fight so that millions can be free, and somehow that makes *you* selfish? Sorry princess, but the world doesn't work that way. You are the most selfless person I know. And, considering I'm an ancient charismatic socialite vampire, I think that's saying something."

I can't help but laugh. "You make it sound so simple. But, it's hard knowing what is right."

He shrugs. "Eh. Only if you overthink it."

Tavian and Kayla find us. "Are you ready to seek the moonlight steel?" asks the traveler.

I think about all that Fen said, and I nod. "Tell me what to do."

...

Tavian guides us deep into the woods, to a place where beams of moonlight fall from the sky, so thick you can run a hand through them, and the wind sings a solemn song. A guardian awaits us there. A great stone beast with wings that do not fly, and eyes that are ever watching. I would call it a gargoyle, but this beast is more majestic than any gargoyle of my mind. It feels eternal.

And it makes me tremble.

"Who seeks the moonlight?" asks the guardian, voice like grinding stone.

Tavian steps forward first. "I do."

The stone creature studies him. "Hmm. A heart of kindness you possess, but too afraid of yourself are you. Too afraid to let others know you. The moonlight, you will not possess."

Tavian bows his head graciously, stepping back. "Thank you, great one."

Kayla steps forward next, her hands firm.

The guardian watches her. "Strong you are, and brave. But torn between two worlds. Are you the Shade, hiding from greatness, or the Druid, leading her people? The moonlight, you will not possess."

Dean taps his chin. "Think I'm seeing a trend here." He steps forward next. "Great stone beast, I believe I am worthy."

The guardian looks at him oddly. Then at us. "Are you serious?"

"Yeah, it was a long shot," says Dean turning back.

Well, that leaves only me.

I step forward, trying to keep my hands from shaking. "I seek the moonlight steel."

The gargoyle bends down, his green eyes on my level. "Interesting. Very interesting. You have a pure heart, but does it know what it wants?" His neck moves like a snake, coiling around me. "You have strength, but can it be controlled?" His stone eyes gaze into mine. "You have courage, but have you ever truly conquered fear?"

He pauses, then pulls away. "The moonlight, you will not possess."

I let out a breath I didn't realize I was holding and turn to my friends. "I'm...I'm sorry."

Dean waves his hand. "Come on, it's not like we did any better."

Kayla crosses her arms as Riku perches on her shoulder preening himself. "I'm starting to doubt anyone can appease this guardian." She points at the gargoyle. "Are you looking for a perfect person, is that it? Well, perfect people don't exist."

The guardian stands taller. His voice booms loudly. "I do not seek one without flaw." He speaks softer. "But one who isn't blind to the truth."

"And what truth would that be?" yells Kayla.

The guardian says nothing.

Yami snuggles against my neck, purring to soothe me. "Thanks, buddy." I say, petting his head. "But, what do we do now?"

Tavian shakes his head. "This I do not know. Without a moonlight sword, we cannot defeat the Darkness."

I sigh, walking away, my tone hardly cheerful. "Well, at least we have a lot of time here, right? Maybe one of us will figure it out."

"Perhaps Marasphyr and Fen should try at least," Dean suggests. "It couldn't hurt."

I'm about to speak, to argue why Fen at least would not pass this test. He is too internally conflicted. But Tavian beats me to it.

"They did not come because they already knew the outcome," he says. "We must find another way."

While the others discuss possible alternatives to our plan, I stroll back to the pond, wishing for a quiet place to think. When I find the pool of water, I see Marasphyr has already taken my rock. "Hey. I think that's my spot. Because—"

Marasphyr isn't responding. Actually, she's clutching her knees to her face and...crying?

I approach her slowly, putting a hand on her back. "What's wrong?"

And just like that, she sits up straight and wipes away the tears. "Nothing. What do you mean?"

I try to be as delicate as possible. "You seem melancholy."

"Do I? Perhaps it's just the lighting." She chuckles at her own joke. Then her voice turns serious. "I saw something. A field of corpses. Thousands dead. I...I can't get it out of my mind."

I sit down beside her. "When did this happen?"

"Just now. Not yet." She smacks her hands against her lap. "Sorry, that doesn't make sense. I see things that have not yet come to pass. Only, it's more like I remember them."

I hadn't really heard much about this power before. "So, it's like you're a fortune teller?"

She rolls her eyes. "Fortune tellers are simply perceptive individuals. What I see is true. Real. But I cannot choose what I remember. It is always random, and often dreadful."

I look into the pond, into my own sad reflection, thinking of what the future may hold. "Have you ever tried to change it? Your visions?"

"Of course," she says. "I could not see a child die and not try to save them. I could not witness a war and not try to stop it. But every time, no matter how hard I tried, or what I did, I changed nothing. My memory would always come to pass. And so, one day I stopped trying. Perhaps it is even why I'm so bitter. Hope seems a false concept to me."

I scoot closer to her, sharing in her woes. "I always hope. But I'm not sure it always matters."

Marasphyr smiles, fidgeting with her ring. "You remind me of myself, you know. A long time ago. Back when things were simpler." She pauses. "You asked me why Inferna is my home. There is a reason. Many millennia ago, before the princes were ever cursed, I was but a small girl growing up in a palace. They called me Merina then. I was the blessed child, heir to all of Ava, the land of my people. But I did not behave blessed. Being blessed meant you had to be sacrificial in all things, putting others before you at all costs, making decisions not for your benefit, but for the benefit of others. I tried for a time. I tried very hard. But some things, like who to love, I could not choose for the sake of others. Things that impassioned me, like discovering new lands, I could not abandon for others. And so, when the time came for me to marry and be queen, I could not. Not on their terms, anyway. And so I was banished. My younger sister became queen, and I was forbidden to swim on Ava again."

I touch her hand. "I'm—"

"Don't be sorry. It happened long ago, as I said. And after my banishment, I explored lands and worlds I couldn't even dream of. I even found love, for a time." She drops her eyes, sighing. "Eventually, I made a home on Inferna. It is a good place for one wishing to be private. And there is a beauty to the land." She looks at me. "I take it, you did not pass the guardian's test?"

"No. Because I don't know what I want." *To return to Inferna, or leave with Fen.*

Marasphyr nods, compassion in her eyes. "I cannot tell you what to want, or what path to follow. But I can tell you that to be torn between two things you love is no way to live."

I pause, thinking on her words. "You wish to travel again, don't you?"

She says nothing.

"But you don't? Is it..." I take a breath, gathering my strength. "Is it because of Fen?"

She looks away. "Like I said, I found love, for a time."

I'm reminded of just how ancient Fen is. How much longer he has lived than me. There are parts of him I may never know. Parts maybe even he has forgotten. We are, in the end, very different beings.

Marasphyr pulls me from my thoughts. "You are with child, are you not?"

I nod, putting a hand on my belly. "Yes."

"Then may I suggest this. Imagine yourself older, your child grown. You tell him or her a story. A story about your greatest regrets. You have many things you would have done differently. But...what makes the top of the list?"

I look down at my belly. "Not saving the Fae."

She smiles. "Then perhaps you have your answer."

I nod, pondering our conversation. I feel different somehow. More certain.

I know what I must do.

I stand and leave Marasphyr by the pond, making my way back through the forest. Until I reach the guardian.

"I seek the moonlight steel," I say, my body still, my mind focused.

The gargoyle bends down, his green eyes peering deeply into mine. "You have a pure heart, but—"

"It wants Fen, and it wants to free the Fae. But if I must choose, it will be the Fae."

His stone neck stretches, examining me from all angles. "You have strength, but—"

"I will learn to control it."

His stone eyes fall back to mine, and he pauses, intent. "You have courage, but—

"I will conquer my fears."

The guardian freezes. For a long while he is silent, his eyes ever watching. "So be it. You know the truth of who you are. The moonlight, you will possess."

And then his eyes close, and he exhales.

It is the last breath he takes.

His stone chest opens, and inside a chunk of steel glows a pale blue. I reach forward and take the moonlight heart.

And now I understand why the test was so difficult. For someone to receive the moonlight steel, the guardian had to die.

12

THE RIFT

"You can look now, Princess. Welcome to hell."

—Asher

I find Tavian and Kayla exiting a cave. They look happy, a little too happy. And they stand close together, as if their bodies orbit each other without conscious intention. Wait a minute...

"You got it!" yells Kayla, pointing at the chunk of moonlight steel in my arms.

"How did you pass the test?" asks Tavian as the back of his hand brushes against Kayla's in a quiet way.

For a moment, I grow sad, thinking about the guardian. "I accepted the truth. I didn't lie to myself." Yami chirps against my hair, nuzzling me.

Tavian nods, pointing at the steel. "Will that be enough for a sword?"

I pass the chunk to Kayla, and she studies it. "Wow. It's extremely light for its size. Yes, this will be enough. Now, I just need tools."

Tavian and I glance at each other. We speak in unison. "Oh..."

I clench my jaw, looking around at the forests and ponds. "Where are we going to find tools here?"

"I know where we can find them in Inferna," says Kayla.

"That must be a last resort," says Tavian, waving his hand. "It will take time to forge the sword, yes? Time we have here. In Inferna, we must be ready for battle."

"I know a place," says a familiar voice. Marasphyr.

Her, Dean, and Fen approach, Baron at their side. Yami jumps down to play with the wolf as I exchange a look with Fen. He smiles. By the Spirits, I just want to grab him and pull him back into that cave. But...there are other things we must do.

Marasphyr studies the moonlight steel and gives me a wink. "There is a place not far from here that will have the tools you need. Come. Follow me quickly."

She leads the way, past flowers of purple and yellow, past great trees and deep caves, past beams of moonlight and shadow.

Then we arrive at a village.

It is a curious place, of houses dug into the ground, and buildings built on trees. It is small, but intricate. And empty.

No one walks the streets. No one makes a sound.

Something dark covers the center of the village. A pit of ash. It smells of smoke and death.

Fen's eyes go cold. "I have seen this before," he says softly, moving forward, studying the pit. He pulls something from the ash. Bits of bone.

My stomach grows queasy and I turn my head, unable to keep in my sickness.

"Someone performed a ritual here," explains Fen, darting a concerned look at me as I wipe at my mouth and right myself. "A ritual to the Darkness."

Tavian looks at Marasphyr, a frown on his face. "Out here? In the Rift?"

She nods. "It seems the Darkness knows no bounds. Anyone may try to summon it."

Fen studies more bones, then draws his sword. "Be wary. The last time Dean and I came to a place like this, the villagers had summoned a Wraith. If you see any survivors, do not trust their words or their faces. It may be the Wraith in disguise."

Everyone nods.

"We must search the houses," continues Fen. "But we must stay together. Tavian, you said the

Wraith is strongest in places of power. Are there any nearby?"

He glances around nervously. "The Rift *is* a place of power."

Fen growls.

I ask him more about this Wraith they encountered, and he explains the details. "She wanted Tavian Gray."

"Why?" I ask.

"Because," says Tavian, his words heavy. "The Darkness cursed me. And so, I must forever flee from its shadow. This curse also makes it nearly impossible for me to fight it."

I don't know why, but Marasphyr scowls at his words.

Then Tavian tells us the rest of his tale. About how he summoned the Darkness, how it killed his family, and the curse it gave him. "There were three of us," he says. "Three who summoned the shadow. Three who paid the price."

"And who are the other two?" asks Fen.

Tavian looks at him, for a moment smiling, and then frowning. "You would not know them."

There is more to this Tavian Gray than he reveals. I step up to him. "Back in Inferna, you used a power I haven't seen before. Your hands shifted into claws. My mentor, Varis, never taught me anything like that."

"He was right not to," says Tavian, brushing back his white fur cloak. "Most Fae have forgotten the old magic. I have not. It is how I can resist Lucian and the Darkness. Most Fae draw power from the four elements, water, earth, fire, and air. But there is another power. Life and death. Light and darkness."

"The Midnight Star," I say.

He nods. "You are right, in a way. Remember Yami is all things. He is the elements and more. Your mentor would have taught you how to tap into the same powers all Fae possess, the powers that connect them to nature. There is a deeper power, but it is dangerous if not controlled properly. I doubt your mentor, Varis, knew how. Few do. And so, it is best he dissuaded you from its use."

I rub my hands together, remembering my time at the Moonlight Gardens. "I didn't always listen. I tried a ritual once to empower Yami. I lost control."

He nods sagely. "Then you have seen how dangerous the old magic can be."

"Yes." I still remember the screams. The burning forest. "That is why...that is why I want you to teach me."

He freezes. "Are you sure this is what you want?"

I stand straighter, gazing into his eyes. "I promised the guardian I will learn control of my powers, and I will."

He doesn't say anything for a while. I notice everyone else has stopped too, looking at us. Hanging on
every word. A tension building between us.

"Very well," says Tavian. "I will teach you." He raises
a finger. "But only as long as it takes Kayla to make the
sword. Then, our training will conclude."

I hold out my hand. "Agreed."

He touches it oddly, slightly shaking it. "By your
human customs, yes. Agreed."

We find nothing in the village. No signs of a Wraith.
And so Kayla seeks out the forge and begins work on the
sword, while Tavian and I train. He teaches me to tap
into my emotions, to control them more than ignore
them. To use them for my own power. It is a difficult
balance, to use rage as fuel and yet not be consumed by
anger. To use sorrow as motivation, and yet not break
down in tears. It takes days before I make any progress.
Days of ignoring everything and everyone except Yami
and Tavian. Days of cutting off my feelings about Fen
because if I spend even a moment fantasizing about
him, I will be lost in those feelings. Because it is so
hard to stay focused in this world, I have to let my training consume me or I will fall into an apathy and ease
I don't understand. But eventually, I notice a shift in
my powers. As my emotions change and weave, so does
Yami. If I control my wrath, he grows in size. If I summon my fear, he grows in speed. My terror brings him

to breathe blue flame. My happiness calms him, turns him small again.

We are not the only ones who train. Fen and Dean spar in the center square, dueling each other for hours on end. Their bodies slick with sweat. Their muscles glistening in the moonlight. Dean struggles to fight his brother at first. But in time, he begins to notice Fen's strategies, his feints and attacks, and he begins to hold his own. The two almost seem a perfect match, until Fen ups the challenge, increasing his speed and disarming Dean quickly. "Better," says the Prince of War. "But not better enough. Again!"

Even Marasphyr takes part in training. She does it privately, away from the rest of us, but sometimes I catch sight of her behind a building, summoning black fire in her hands, conjuring portals. Once, she notices me, and stops immediately. "Don't you have things to practice?" she snaps.

I leave her alone and resume my studies. Tavian proves a much faster teacher than Varis. One time, I ask him why that might be. "You must understand," says Tavian, drawing glyphs in the sand between us with a stick. "The Druids were never meant to train the Midnight Star. It was a skill passed down from one High Fae to another. The Midnight Star would, in his or her lifetime, train all the children in the family, preparing them for the day one of them might be chosen. If the

Midnight Star died early, their siblings also possessed the knowledge, and would take on training the younglings." He waves his hands in the air, having me mimic his movements. "So you see, when the High Fae were all slaughtered, their art was lost with them. Knowledge of the old magic faded."

I raise an eyebrow. "But, what about you? How do you know this power then?"

He smiles. "I knew a Midnight Star once. She was… very dear to me. You have her eyes, you know."

My green eyes. A reminder of a family I never knew. "What happened to her?"

Tavian looks down in the sand, seeing something I do not. "She died. In a great battle, between Fae and vampire."

"You mean…" My eyes go wide. "You mean you knew my aunt?"

"Yes." He beams at me fondly. "We grew up together. Playing in the ancient groves. Pulling tricks on the Druids. She was a fierce person, your aunt, full of courage and passion. She was like you, really."

"What was her name?"

He breathes deeply, like savoring a good taste. "Saphira."

"Saphira," I repeat, committing the name to memory.

"She had deep blue hair, and a smile that would make anyone blush. I…I never told her how I felt. And then, the war began, and it was too late."

I touch his hand. "How did she die?"

"Like a hero," he says. "In a great battle. The entire forces of the Fae met the entire forces of the vampire. Lucian and Saphira dueled for days. In the end, she won, and then, she did something I could never do. She showed mercy. Mercy to the vampire king. A chance to surrender. He took advantage of the moment, and cut her hand with his sword. One cut is all it took. There was some kind of poison on the blade, and Saphira fell, her body shaking with spams, her face turning blue. I did not reach her in time. But I held her corpse in my arms, weeping as the Fae lost their freedom."

He rips up a blade of grass, twirling it in his fingers. "I found love again, as you know. Many years later. I had a family. But in my dreams, I still danced with Saphira. I still held her in my arms. I never forgot. And so one day, when the opportunity arose, I joined a rebellion. There had been other uprisings before, but this one, this one had a true leader. A man who could truly bring peace between vampire and Fae. The Moonlight Prince they called him. He led with courage. Dispensed justice with grace. He was...too angry, at the time, but I did not realize. I too was full of rage. Together, we concocted a plan. A way to defeat the vampires once and for all. And so we summoned the Darkness. And what a dreadful price we paid."

I scoot closer. "What happened to the prince?"

Tavian chuckles, but there's no warmth to it. "Haven't you heard? He disappeared."

Something tickles at my mind. "You said there were three, before. Three cursed. Who was the third?"

He pauses for a long while. "The third—"

"It's ready," says Kayla, walking over, beaming with pride, Riku chirping on her shoulder. "Come. See for yourself."

Tavian sighs, and whispers in my ear. "The third is dead." Then he says no more.

Together, we follow Kayla to the forge.

Once there, she hands me the most beautiful sword I have ever seen. It glows a pale blue and feels cold to the touch. Ancient Fae glyphs are etched into the steel and drawn onto the leather hilt. I wave the blade through the air, noting its light weight, its perfect balance. This is a sword kingdoms would wage war over. A sword people would die for.

"What will you call it?" asks Kayla.

I study the moonlight blade, remembering the guardian who gave his life. "I'll call it Lux. It means light in Latin. And with this light, I will defeat the Darkness." I gaze into my blade for a long moment, seeing the heart of the guardian who sacrificed for it. "It is time. Time to end this war."

Tavian shakes his head. "Your training is not yet complete."

"But you said..." a memory tickles my mind, growing fuzzier by the moment..."you said..."

"I said we have time here. Much time to prepare. We must not rush to battle."

Right. A year here is just a handful of days in Inferna. We can stay longer, train longer. I'll only have one chance to defeat Lucian. I need to be at my best. My hand falls to my stomach, a thought slipping through my mind like sand through a clenched fist. There's something I'm supposed to remember. Something I can't forget.

But Tavian pulls me into another training session, while Kayla begins a new project: forging a set of armor from scraps found in the village. Fen and Dean continue sparing. Days pass. We live in our own little bubbles, focusing on the things that matter to us most, but forgetting why they matter at all.

One day, as we sit in a tree house, as I carve the ancient glyphs into the wooden floor, I hear the slow rising of breath and...snoring? "Tavian, are you sleeping?"

His eyes pop open. He adjusts his position, his legs crossed in lotus. "No. No. Continue your training. Recite the primal emotions."

"But that's what we did last time. And the time before."

He raises an eyebrow. "Is it?" He shrugs. "Oh well. Maybe you practice whatever you wish today. We can resume lessons tomorrow. It's just so...so peaceful here." He leans back and falls asleep once more.

I jump and grab his shoulders, shaking him. "Tavian. Tavian wake up! We don't have time to mess around."

He mutters half-asleep. "But we do. We have all the time we need."

Something is seriously wrong. With him. With me. I shake my head, trying to clear it. We need to focus. Yami is curled around my neck in his own peaceful slumber, and I can't remember the last time he played with Baron or explored the flowers. I look around the treehouse for something to cause a racket, and then I see the glyphs. Hundreds of them, carved into the floor, the walls, a spider web of symbols. How long have I been studying the same thing over and over?

I try to wake Tavian once more to no avail, so I run out the treehouse and find Kayla by the forge. She sits next to the anvil, a blade of grass between her teeth. Her phoenix, Riku, perches on a tree branch near her, looking as dazed and sleepy as everyone else.

Kayla looks up, her eyes unfocused. "Arianna! How are you?"

"Something's wrong with Tavian. He's not waking."

She looks at me oddly. "Then let him sleep. He probably just needs rest."

I run my hands through my hair, trying to keep myself from exploding. Doesn't she see the problem? "We don't have time to sleep all day. We need to get back to Inferna."

She nods thoughtfully, but says nothing.

I sigh. "How's the armor going?"

"The armor? Oh, the armor. Yes, it's almost done. It's right over there."

I follow her gaze to the workstation. Upon it lie a few scraps of metal, some of them nailed together in odd angles. "This...this is just junk."

"Hey. Hey. That's a real work of art in the making." Kayla tries to stand, then seems to decide against it.

I walk back over to her. "Well, how much longer do you need to finish it?"

She shrugs. "A couple days maybe. I don't know. You can't rush perfection."

I frown at her, with my are-you-serious face.

She waves her hands. "Fine. Fine. I'll work on it some right now."

"Thank you."

She stands sluggishly, grabbing a hammer, and walks over to the workstation. "Now where did I leave... ah, here." She picks up a small nail, positions it on the armor with care, and hammers it in. "There! A good day's work."

"By the Spirits, what is going on?" I whisper.

Kayla walks back to the anvil and resumes her sitting. "You know, it was good seeing you. You should come back tomorrow. I should have more done by then."

I groan and storm off, searching for the one person who couldn't possibly be calm.

I find Fen sitting in the courtyard, sharpening his sword with a stone, Baron sleeping at his heel. The prince wears no shirt, his muscles rippling in the unnatural light. I try not to stare, but well, I stare. "Where's Dean. I thought the two of you were sparring?"

"We were, but then our blades grew dull. No fun that way."

"And how long have you been sharpening that sword, exactly?"

He shrugs. "It could always be sharper."

I bend down and touch my finger to the steel. "Ouch." I pull back, studying the drop of blood on my hand, and showing it to Fen. "Looks sharp enough."

"Could always be sharper."

By the Spirits, I want to smack him. "Look, Fen. Something weird is happening here. Everyone has grown lazy."

"Not you."

No. Not me. At least, not as much. Something makes me different, lets me keep track of time better. "Listen, Fen." I grab his hands, stopping his bloody sharpening, and make him face me. "I'm going back to Inferna. To free the Fae. I need you. I need you by my side."

He blinks, and something changes in his eyes. They grow darker, more focused. "War breeds war. This is not the way."

"But some battles are worth fighting."

He squeezes my hands tighter. "Come with me. Back to Earth. Let us raise our child together."

"I want to. I want to so much. But I can't, not yet. First, we need to stop the Darkness."

The focus fades then. His eyes turn dim. He pulls away, leans back and grinds the stone against his sword. "Perhaps once my blade is sharper."

My eye well with tears, and I bite down on my hand to stop myself from crying out. This place has changed him. Or perhaps...perhaps it was the month we spent apart, while I was kept prisoner on Grey Mountain. Maybe we grew distant. I don't know what to think anymore.

I run off, looking for someone, anyone, who knows what the hell is going on. Deep in the woods, I hear him before I see him. Dean. He lies in a grove, plucking petals off a flower. "She loves me. She loves me not. She loves me—"

"Dean, I need your—" I notice the open field behind him. Thousands of petals and dead flowers cover the grass. How long have we been here?

Dean seems to notice me for the first time. "Ah, princess. Care for a roll in the hay, or the field, as it were?"

I shake my head. "No. Of course, not."

"If it's Fen you're worried about, don't. I haven't seen him for weeks."

Weeks? I thought we'd only been here a few days.

I grab Dean by the shoulders and make him face me. "Listen, Dean. We need to leave. Return to Inferna."

He waves his hand dismissively. "Right. Right. After your training is done and all."

I grip him tighter. "My training *is* done."

He chuckles. "Silly girl. Training's never done. You could always be better."

Okay. I can't take this anymore. I raise my hand. And smack him across the face.

"What the—"

I smack him again.

He bounces back, his eyes wide. "Bloody hell princess, I didn't know you liked it rough."

Smack.

Smack.

Smack.

He grabs by hand. "Fine. Enough already. I get the point. You want serious Dean. Well, you have him."

I let go off my breath, unclenching my fist. "Finally. Okay, Dean, something is going on. Everyone's lost in a haze. They're barely doing anything, just repeating worthless actions."

He grimaces. "Well, not me. I've been practicing with Fen. Getting better too, I might say. I just came out here for a short break, to pick the flowers."

I point him to the field of a thousand dead petals.

He rubs his chin, seemingly thinking. "Well, I do have super speed at my disposal."

I punch his shoulder. "You weren't picking these flowers at super speed. I saw you. It was more molasses speed. In fact, molasses would have laughed at you."

He sucks in air sharply. "Oh. That's bad. How long have we been here?"

I cross my arms. "I don't know. But I do know someone who will."

"The mermaid?"

I nod. "Let's go see her."

"Yes. You go ahead. I'll just—"

"Oh no." I grab his hand. "You're coming with me, serious Dean. Before molasses Dean returns."

"Come on. Things can't really be that bad."

"Really?" I put my hands on my hips. "When was the last time you had a drink? When was the last time you *lay* with someone?"

Dean's jaw drops. "Holy baby demon. We need to get out of here now!"

Together, we run out of the forest. We find Marasphyr by the pond, sitting on a rock, brushing her hair with a comb from the village. I step forward, my tone firm. "Either you've been brushing your hair non-stop for who knows how long, or you have some explaining to do. And I gotta say, that hair doesn't look all that neat."

She chuckles, putting the brush down. "I see you have become aware of the Rift's magic, of how it soothes and calms."

"And how it makes everyone lazy. What is it, some kind of spell?"

She taps her fingers on the rock. "In part, it is magic yes. But psychological also. Think how much of life is driven by urgency, by a sense of time running out. Here there is no time. No urgency. No deadlines."

I sigh, her words sinking in. "And so there's no reason to finish anything. Ever."

She picks up the brush again and combs her hair. "Exactly. But there are perks too. No pressure. No responsibility."

I grab the damn brush and toss it aside. "This is the real reason you brought us here, isn't it? So you can stay here forever with Fen. So you can keep him trapped."

Dean whistles. "Oh, that's messed up. Even for me."

Marasphyr doesn't seem phased, her composure pristine. "If someone truly wishes to leave this place, it's not difficult. The Rift would open a portal for them. That is how this place works. Tavian stays because here he can sleep in peace, away from the politics of the world. Kayla stays to be with Tavian, and to avoid the responsibilities of a Druid. And you know why Fenris stays. I heard him tell you."

My anger leaves me. My limbs grow cold. "He doesn't wish to be king," I whisper.

Marasphyr smiles, and what a twisted smile it is.

I draw my sword, Lux, and point it at the witch. "You will take us out of here. You will summon a portal, and I'll push everyone through if I have to. We will leave together."

She laughs. "Do not threaten me girl. I have killed kings and slain empresses. I have even fought a Midnight Star before."

Dean draws his sword as well. "You know, I thought things could work out between us, Marasphyr. I really did. But I think we need a break. And it's not me. It's you." He strikes at the mermaid.

She waves her hand.

And then...

She's gone.

Vanished in a puff of smoke.

What did she—

"Looking for me," Marasphyr calls from above. She sits in a tree, grinning. She waves her hand again, and suddenly she's standing on the other side of the pond. Then she's leaning against an old oak. "You will never catch me. Never beat me. So let's not play this game, as fun as it may be."

She's right. Trying to force her to do anything will be a waste of time. And trying to convince the others to leave has been futile. "How long have we been here, truly?" I ask. "How much time has passed in Inferna?"

"Let me see..." she clicks her tongue, mimicking a clock. "It'd say we've been here two months. Maybe three. So that's about a day in Inferna. Maybe a little more."

Months. Whole months. My hand falls to my stomach, where my baby is growing, and I feel my normally flat stomach now gently curved. I have a baby bump, I realize, surprised. How could I not have noticed my own baby growing inside of me? This is what has tethered me to time. My child. While no one else in the Rift changed over past days and weeks, being the immortals they are, I *have* changed. My child has changed. We've grown.

And we can't waste any more time.

"I will return," I say. "Once I've defeated the Darkness, I will return with an army and free my friends."

Marasphyr rolls her eyes. "Whatever you say." And then, for a brief moment, she turns serious. "I do want you to win, you know. I really do."

"Well, you have an odd way of helping us."

She looks down, quiet. And I realize she is torn again. Torn between staying with Fen and going off on adventure. She is like me, before I passed the test with the guardian.

I say no more. No more needs to be said.

It's time to go.

But first...I look down at my hand, at the ring Fen had made for me when I first came to Stonehill. I slip it off my finger and study it. "Marasphyr, I know you have no love for me, but I must ask you one last favor." I hold out the ring. "Can you please give this to Fen? Tell him...well...just give him the ring. I've already said what I needed to say."

Marasphyr opens her hand and I lay the ring on her palm. She stares at it a moment with a guarded expression on her face. Then she clutches it in her fingers and nods. "I will do as you ask, Arianna Spero. And I wish you the Spirit's luck on your journey."

I grab Dean's hand and close my eyes. Let's see if Marasphyr was being honest.

I want to leave. I want to leave. I want...

I open my eyes.

And see a mountain before me. The Rift is gone, and my head is clear. The calmness, the peace that permeated The Rift has left me. Though I wasn't as affected as the others, I still feel a heaviness settle on me. The weight of responsibility. The weight of consequence. But rather than suffer under that weight, I now relish it. Value it. It is the feeling of purpose. The feeling of a life that can make a difference.

I see a shift in Dean as well, as he wraps his arms around himself to block out the chill in the air. His features are less dreamy, more solid, more serious—at least as serious as the Prince of Lust gets. "Where are we?" he asks.

"Grey Mountain," I say, petting Yami on my shoulder. "I left something here."

The underground dwellings have been abandoned. The Fae probably moved on to fight for Lucian, and so it's easy to scour the rooms. Eventually, I find what was taken from me. My armor, half black and half white. And Spero.

"What now?" asks Dean.

"Now," I say, raising my two swords. "We fly to Ace's realm. And then the real war begins."

13

ACE

"Ace is brilliant. He's also lazy, or so he says."
—Fenris Vane

I focus my emotions, summoning my anger, and Yami roars. He dematerializes into black dust, and then the dust takes on a new, larger form, the size of a gryphon. I jump on Yami's back, holding onto one of his black spikes, and offer my hand to Dean. "Come on. We have no time to lose."

He's frozen. Awe on his face. But then he shakes his head, grabs my arm and hops on behind me, wrapping his arms around my waste. "I think I dreamed about this once," he says mischievously. "It had a happy ending."

I roll my eyes. "I imagine all your dreams have happy endings," I say with a smirk.

I expect a chuckle and some witty response, but instead he sighs and holds me tighter. "Not all, Princess."

I want to ask him what he means, but I have to focus on the task at hand. I will Yami to move.

He unfolds his giant wings, and with one burst of power, we lunge into the air, spiraling through the clouds. The experience of flight fills me with joy, with peace, and I savor the moment while I can.

"You know," says Dean, looking down, "I think everyone should have a dragon. Think you can get me one? Maybe if Yami has babies or something?"

"That's not how it works with Spirits."

"Pity." He sighs. "A life is truly incomplete without a baby dragon."

"I'll have to agree with you there," I say, petting Yami's head and scratching behind his horns.

We fly near lands full of raging water, with giant stones jutting from the earth beneath us.

"Zeb's realm," says Dean. "I don't see any fires below. Hopefully, that's a good sign."

Hopefully.

Dean lays his head on my shoulder, his voice soft. "We really are going to go back for the others, right? I'm kind of fond of my little brother."

"I'm fond of Fen, too," I say with a bit of snarkiness. "And yes, if we must, we will go back."

"If?"

"We may not have to return to the Rift. Because I hope…I hope that when our friends realize we're gone, they'll leave to find us. That Fen will leave to find me."

A breath. "And what if he doesn't?"

I don't think about that. I dare not.

We press on. To a realm of yellow rocks and sparse shoots of grass. A realm of cliffs and canyons. The Realm of Sloth. In the distance stands a grand city. It is surrounded by walls and watched over by a fortress.

I whisper under my breath, casting illusion, making us all translucent and blending us with the night sky. If nothing else, the incessant and repetitive training with Tavian has drilled spells and magic into me so deeply I could do it in my sleep, and to some degree was. This training is a part of me in ways I still don't fully realize. I have become truly one with my magic. Silently, we glide past the walls and land in an empty square. People must be in their homes at this late hour. That or...I don't allow myself to think of the alternative. Ace *must* still be in control of this realm. He must.

We dismount, and I summon my happiness, turning Yami smaller. He jumps up on my shoulder and snuggles against my neck.

"Follow me," says Dean. "I know the way to the fortress."

We walk down a street, and I quickly realize this city is far larger than I even thought. It's funny how small things can look from up in the sky. Down here, everything looms over me. A few minutes pass, and people start to leave their homes, setting up shops, tending to jobs. I note their fancy clothing and clear eyes. Vampires. Good. The sun begins to rise, though the sky turns barely brighter. It seems we must live in Darkness while Lucian still draws breath.

I allow myself to look around, to enjoy this place I've never visited before.

The Realm of Sloth is truly a place of marvels. Golden carriages ride on rails throughout the city, taking nobles to grand halls and splendid manors, while others with less fortune travel by canal or on foot, filling up giant market squares where goods and inventions are traded. Green vines spill over the golden buildings, and glass doors and ceilings are common, filling the city with the dull hue of a diluted sun blocked by Darkness. It's all very steampunk fantasy, at least according to the standards of my own world. It's funny how far away that seems. I haven't thought about social media or cell phones or cat videos in so long. Everything about me has changed. I guess it's part of survival that we so easily adapt to the circumstances in which we find ourselves. That and maybe there's something in my blood that always knew this place, this world was part of me. Steam contraptions pop and fizzle on the sidewalks, creating juicy drinks one can purchase on the go. Dean buys me one, and I find the taste a mix of pineapple and something unique to this realm, something that makes me tingle. Then we reach the fortress.

The Golden Castle stands atop a hill surrounded by canals, its golden walls shooting up into the sky, filled with trebuchets ready to fire at enemy forces and soldiers prepared to fight off any invaders. It is larger than High Castle, Sky Castle, even Stonehill. Pathways connect it to the giant walls spanning the entire city. Dean explains the reasoning, waving his hands in grand gestures. "The gates can be reinforced with troops straight from the castle. For the metropolis to fall, the fortress must fall. This was not the way with Stonehill, where too often the city was ruined while the castle stood strong. Here, civilians are safe during battle. Ace is a bloody genius, I tell you."

We reach the castle gates, and the guards, two men clad in golden armor, recognize Dean instantly. "Prince Dean. We'd heard reports your realm had fallen to the Fae. We thought you were..."

"Alive and well, as you can see," he says with a smile and a wink. "We must see Prince Ace immediately."

"Of course, but..."

Dean clenches his jaw. "But?"

"He's in an important meeting."

Dean and I exchange glances. Important meeting? Lucian said he would offer his children a chance to pledge allegiance. If that's what happening now..."We must get to him immediately," I say, drawing my two swords. "Take us to him now, or else face a vampire prince and the Midnight Star."

Their eyes go wide at the mention of my title. "Of course, Prince all Powerful. This way."

Dean chuckles as the guards open the gate, and we follow them inside, up golden stairs and hallways until we reach a grand door. I push it open, swords at the ready in case Ace proves foe rather than ally.

The Prince of Sloth stands by his war table, a brown cloak falling from his shoulders, a belt of gadgets strapped to his waist. A clock-like gizmo hangs on his wrist, and a sword hangs at his side. He no longer wields the cane. His face is hard. Eyes like brown marble. Dark brown hair neat. This is not the injured Ace I last saw, but a prince ready for war.

A familiar face is with him. Zeb leans over a map, his shady hair messy, his eyes too tired. So, this is who Ace was meeting with.

Tension hangs in the air between us.

Last time I saw these two, the council sentenced Fen and I to death. Now, I need their help.

I step forward. "Ace, I—"

He raises a hand, cutting me off. "Before you speak your part, I must know one thing. The thing I have asked myself every day of this past month. Why did you never tell me the truth? Why did you never tell me you were the Midnight Star?"

Dean reaches for his sword, but I touch his hand and shake my head. "I will tell you." I see in Ace's eyes only the truth will do. Another lie will break him. I step forward once more, closer to the two princes. "First, the Fae...no, Lucian, forced me into a new contract. I could not speak the truth to anyone who didn't already know it. I could not tell you I was the Midnight Star. I could not even tell you your father still lived. If I tried, my mouth would lock shut, my body would fill with pain."

Zeb looks away, his face reflecting the agony of my words. Ace gives me no sign. No change in his mood.

I step closer, continuing. "So I could not tell you, even if I wanted to. Not until the battle at Stonehill. The contract was terminated so that I could defend myself even if it meant revealing I was Fae. It is then, of course, you found out the truth. A part of me wishes you had known sooner." I step closer once more. "But in the end, even if I could have told you earlier, I do not think I would have. You are my friend, yes, but you are also a prince. You have a responsibility to your people. A duty to protect them. If you had to choose between me and your realm, I suspect you would pick your people in the end. I think, if you would not, then we would never have been friends."

For the first time, Ace responds, his face softening. "You are not wrong," he says quietly.

Zeb stands taller. "I would have chosen my people as well."

I nod. "And that is why we are alike. I don't know if you can forgive me, both of you. Perhaps you will one day. But right now, no matter what you think of me, we are still bound together by what we believe. Our people are in danger, and we choose to protect them above all else."

Zeb and Ace exchange a look, their jaws tense.

Dean approaches his brothers. "I have travelled with Arianna these past few months, and I swear to you, she has always had the best interests of both Fae and vampire at heart. She seeks nothing but peace and freedom for both our kind."

Zeb looks at me, scanning me up and down. "We have not known each other long, princess, but I remember when you and Fen visited my realm for food and talk. I sensed in you then what I sense in you now. The will to do good." He turns to Ace. "I trust her, brother."

The Prince of Sloth points to the map. "Even if we were to fight with you, how can we win? Levi, Niam, and even Asher have pledged alliance to Lucian. As we speak, they march with an army of thousands—vampire, Shade, and Fae—toward the Realm of Gluttony. They will take it in three days' time."

I point to a shallow crossing on the map, a place where the river grows thin enough to walk over. "They will have to pass through here. We meet them with your combined armies and force them into battle."

"We don't have the numbers to win," says Zeb.

"We don't need to beat their army," I say. "We just need to beat Lucian. Once the king is dead, the Fae will no longer fight against us."

Ace shakes his head. "No one can defeat our father. No one but his brother."

"I know of another who did defeat him," I say. "A Midnight Star. But she showed mercy, and Lucian killed her. I will not repeat the same mistake."

Zeb sits on the table, crossing his legs. "I had heard rumors, but they were always dismissed. Few saw the final battle between Lucian and the High Fae. The official story is he overpowered her with ease, but if what you say is true…"

"I can kill him," I say, clutching my sword. "I swear it."

Ace grimaces. "And what of the creature? The beast of Darkness he keeps at his heel?"

Dean throws his arms around his brothers' shoulders'. "Surely the three of us can find a way to separate them? We draw the creature away with our forces, and Arianna fights good old daddy."

"This seems a fool's plan," says Ace. "I would rather join with Lucian than see all my people slaughtered."

He turns away, studying the map. "What of Fenris? Why is he not with you?"

Dean raises his hands, fumbling for words. "He..."

"He's tired of fighting," I say. "Tired of ruling." I don't tell them the rest, that I suspect Fen said the things he did in part because of the Rift. I don't wish to waste time.

Zeb paces, then sighs. "It may be a fool's plan. But it's the only one we have. And I, for one, am not pledging allegiance to Lucian. He wishes to fight the heavens and force his brother to break our curse, and yet he hasn't considered the cost. I remember how we battled the angels. I remember how friends I had grown up with, women I had loved, I remember how they all died before my eyes. And even worse, I remember the friends who killed them, those people who sided against us. We lost to the heavens before. And we will lose again." He jabs his finger at the map. "I say we stand a better chance to win this battle right now, then to try and break the curse with Lucian. Ace, brother, you must see this."

Ace doesn't respond.

So Zeb reaches around him, to a silver platter and grabs a...cupcake?

He eats it voraciously as everyone stares. Then another. And another. He speaks between chews. "Together..." Chew. Chew. "We will..." Chew. Chew. "Defeat." Chew. Chew. "The Darkness." He pauses from his consumption of treats, noticing my wide eyes. "What?" he asks. "It's the curse. I swear."

Dean whispers in my ear. "You get used to this after a while."

Ace sighs like an overworked parent, then offers me his hand. "I need you to see something."

I can tell by his gaze this can't wait, so I take his hand and follow him to the door.

Dean walks behind us.

"Only her," says Ace.

Dean grabs the hilt of his sword. "Not sure I trust the two of you alone."

Ace gestures all around him. "Brother, you are in my fortress, surrounded by thousands of my soldiers. I don't need to lead her into a trap, because you are already trapped if I wish it. Understand?"

Dean looks around, his face suddenly nervous. "Well, bloody hell, when you put it that way."

"We won't be gone long," says Ace. "In the meantime, prepare for battle."

Zeb heads for the exit. "I shall return to my realm at once and gather my army. We suffered casualties fending off the Fae, but there are still many of us. We shall meet your army at the river crossing. I will take position behind the hill. When you send a signal, we will strike at Lucian's force from the flank, breaking his army."

"The signal must be easy to spot," says Ace.

I nudge the little dragon on my shoulder. "I will send the signal. Yami will shoot blue fire straight into the sky."

Zeb nods. "Very well. Then I will see you tomorrow. When we win, I'm buying everyone a round of drinks." He runs out, his footsteps echoing in the halls.

I motion to Dean. "I'll be fine. Prepare the soldiers."

He nods, but doesn't move.

I follow Ace through a small door, down an empty hallway. "When the Fae lost control," I ask, "how did you fare?"

"At first it was chaos. Fae slaughtering Shade and vampire in the streets. But once we understood the problem, I sent my best men to stop the uprising. I ordered them to capture whenever possible. The dungeons are full now, but I wish we could have saved more." He opens a door and leads me through.

Inside lie a variety of golden trinkets, old and dusty. Pots, platters, statuettes. But one trinket catches my eye immediately. "A mirror."

Ace grins. "Each prince keeps one in secret, for—"

"For emergencies, I know. So, where are we going?"

He grabs my hand and leads me forward. "A place you know very well, Princess."

...

We step out into a bathroom. The floor is dirty. The sink filled with snot. The walls...familiar. This is..."This is the bathroom at the Roxy."

"Yes. It's close enough to where we need to go." Ace adjusts his hair in the mirror, straightening it.

"Um," I point at his cape and gadgets. "You know you'll stand out, right?"

He frowns at me. "You're none better," he says.

I look down at my very medieval looking white gown and the two swords I carry. At least Yami is hidden as a dragon necklace. "You're right. I won't blend in either."

He freezes. "Right, well, I'll just say it's Halloween."

"But it's not."

He raises an eyebrow. "What do you mean?"

"You can't just say it's Halloween. It has to be the actual day."

"Really? Your human customs are so strange."

He turns to the sink to wash his hands.

I sigh. "Okay, we can say we're part of a fantasy game reenactment. Cosplay. That should give us a good cover."

"Cosplay?" he says, holding the word in his mouth like a foreign thing he's afraid to taste.

"Yeah, it's when humans dress up like characters from their favorite..." Ace's eyes are vacant and he looks bored. I sigh again. "Nevermind. Just let me do the talking if anyone questions our choice of clothing."

He washes his hands, then gestures at the door. "After you."

I lead, entering a place I once called a second home. Everything is familiar, everything makes me feel welcome. Jesus eyeing the naked sculptures. The Neon signs. The baby bottles filled with milk for customers' coffee.

"Oh, Ari, sweetie. I didn't see you come in." Sheri runs up to me, wrapping me in a hug. "It's been so long. How have you been? And who's this dashing young man?"

Ace raises his cape in front of his eyes. "It's Halloween."

"No…no…" I shake my head and pull his cape down. "He's a friend. I'm just showing him the sights."

"You want to grab a bite to eat?"

I wear my best sorry face. "Actually, I just wanted to drop by and say high. We have a bus to catch."

"Well drop by more often, okay? You're family here."

"I will." I hug her quickly and smile as Ace pulls me toward the exit, but I pause for one moment, looking at Sheri, in case…in case it's the last time I see her. "Thank you," I say. "For everything." And then we leave. It's night, of course, for the sun on this world would harm Ace. A light rain falls.

Ace leads me to an old apartment, where the walls are covered in graffiti and the air smells of vomit. He leads me up a flight of stairs to the second floor and knocks on a green door at the very back of the hallway.

An elderly woman opens the door, her grey hair wrapped in a bun, her face kindly. "Master Ace," she says, hugging him. "It's been so long."

He chuckles. "Too long. Is she awake?"

"Yes. Was just about to put her to bed."

"Would this be a good time?"

"Oh, of course, of course." She shuffles out of the way, letting us inside the apartment. The walls are painted red. A thick ornate carpet covers the floor. A brown plush couch sits in the living room, opposite a roaring fireplace. Clearly, this place is a step above the rest of the building. A few steps actually.

In the corner sits a little girl, around eight, stacking wooden blocks. When she looks up, her face lights up. "Uncle Ace!" She jumps up and runs into his arms, hugging him fiercely.

"Hey pumpkin," he says, kissing her cheek. "How have you been?"

"I've been great," she says with grand gestures. "Want to help me build a tower?"

"Sure," says the prince. And then he sits with the little girl, and together they build a tower out of blocks.

I try to figure out what's happening here, but this... this is the last thing I expected.

"Patricia," says Ace. "Patricia. I have someone for you to meet." Ace motions me over to the girl. To Patricia. "Patricia. This is Ari, a dear friend of mine. Ari, this is Patricia."

"So nice to meet you," I say, sitting down beside them.

"Nice to meet you, too," says Patricia. Her hair is long and brown and messy. Her eyes are dark brown. "You want to help us build?" I nod, and she continues. "I think we should make a castle next. But they are much harder than towers. We must make sure we have the proper foundation. Here. Let me show you how."

She guides me through the process while Ace watches, his face the happiest I have seen. We work long into the night. And when I ask Patricia to pass a block, I realize she is asleep. Ace lifts her up and puts her to bed as I watch from the doorway. He kisses her on the forehead, and sings her a song about a princess looking for home. I have never heard Ace sing before. His voice is deep and gentle. A soothing one to fall asleep to.

When the song is finished, he kisses Patricia one last time, and leaves the room, closing the door behind him. He speaks softly to me. "Do you understand now, what I have to lose?"

I think on the entire night, the pieces clicking together in my mind. "She's your daughter, isn't she?"

He nods. "I loved a woman once. A long time ago. But we...we couldn't be together. Our worlds were too different. So we decided to stay apart. But one day, one day my love returned, and she told me of our child." He sits down on the couch, gazing into the fireplace. "Until that moment, I didn't realize how much I wanted to be a father. How much joy it could bring. I still remember the first time I met her, how she wrapped her hand around my finger and stared into my eyes. I vowed then that I would keep her safe. That I would never let any harm fall upon her." He pauses. "Patricia is not a full vampire. Her blood, like your blood, tempts my kind. It makes us see you as inferior. And I could not...I could not subjugate her to that fate."

"So you kept her secret," I say. "But why not turn her?"

"And curse her?" he asks. "So that the sun burns her? So that she craves blood above all else? No. I would not wish this upon anyone. Not even my worst enemies."

I sit next to him, holding his hand. "Where is her mother?"

"Gone somewhere I do not know," he says, his eyes turning red. "Her life, her life was not that of a mother's. My life not that of a father's. So I brought Patricia here, where Old Meg takes care of her, raises her, teaches her the things she needs to know. I visit when I can. Less and less frequently these past few months."

"Why not stay here always?" I ask. "I know I would do anything for my child. Even give up a realm."

He nods, picking at a seam on his brown cloak. "I would give up my realm. I would give up even all my inventions. But what I cannot do, what I will not do, is hurt Patricia. If I stay here, if I let her know who I truly am, she will care for me all the deeper. And I for her. And yet, I could not give her all she deserves. I could not be with her during the day. If she ever got a cut and bled, I could not help her. I would have to leave just to keep control of my senses. I would have to abandon her at times she needs me most." He clenches his fist, gazing into the fire. "I hate this curse. I hate it more than I have ever hated anything. It keeps me from remembering all the wondrous things I see here. It keeps me from the woman I love. It keeps me from my daughter."

"Perhaps," I say, my voice soft, "she would prefer a father, one who spends even a little time with her, over an uncle who barely visits."

Tears well in his eyes, and he turns away. His voice breaks with sobs. "We are of the same blood yes, but I'm not her father. I'm not here enough to be her father. But I wish I could be. I wish it with all my being." He turns to me, his eyes full of sorrow. "Whatever happens tomorrow, we must win. Because I must return to her. I must return, do you understand?"

I take his hand in my own. "I understand. But I cannot promise victory. All I can promise is that I will do my best. That I will fight until the end."

He glances back at the door, back where Patricia sleeps. "Then that will have to be enough."

14

MOONLIGHT PRINCE

"There were three of us. Three who summoned
the shadow. Three who paid the price."
—Tavian Gray

PART I

—Arianna Spero—

After we leave his daughter, we make one more stop
before returning to Inferna. To the hospital where
my mother's body is being cared for. I step into the
sterile room, where the whir of machines keep her
alive. I put a hand over hers and let the tears that
fill my eyes fall down my face. "I could save you easily, if I did as Fen asked. If I just left with him. But
I hope you understand. This isn't just about you and
me anymore. This is about a whole world of people. I

can't abandon them to their fate, not when I have the power to make it different."

She doesn't answer, of course. But I think somewhere, somehow she hears me. As I leave I ask the nurse for a piece of paper and pen, and I write a short letter to Es and Pete. Just in case. Because the future is uncertain, and this battle might be my last. "Could you mail this for me?" I ask the nurse.

She's about to say no, that it's not their policy to play postal service to patients, but then something shifts in her face. Maybe she sees into something deeper, something truer than rules. Because her face softens and she nods. "I can't do it from work, but I'll drop it by the post office after."

I smile at her, touched by her kindness, by her willingness to go out of her way for a stranger.

And as I turn to leave, I stop again, something tugging at my mind. "There was a man here before; he visited my mom. Has he been here again?"

Ace paces the floor impatiently, but the nurse, she pauses, a curious expression overtaking her face. "Actually, yes, there was someone. He left a note, said to give it to anyone who asked about him."

She rummages through my mother's file and pulls out a small envelope, handing it to me. "It's all very strange," she says with a vague expression on her face. And I wonder if she's been influenced by magic.

I open the note as we leave. It isn't long, but it is life-altering.

Dear Ari,

If you're reading this, then you remember seeing me. That in itself is something. It means you're growing in your powers.

I have so much to apologize for, but I fear I haven't the time. I know what Inferna and Avakiri are going through. I know what has become of you all.

I wish I could have been the father you needed. The father you deserved.

But I faced a different fate.

In punishment for my rebellion, I was cursed to be a guardian of power. A gift and a curse some might say.

I was banished to another realm, turned to stone to guard a powerful magic.

I was allowed one grace: that I could, once every circling of the moon, take on my human form and return to earth. It is there I met your mother. There we fell in love and conceived you. There I had to let you go. To protect you. To protect her. To fulfill my duty, my curse, my fate.

I sense our fates will cross again. And this time, I will be ready to give you what you need.

My love is with you always.

Your father

I drop the paper and it flutters to the linoleum hospital floor as I stand in shock. I still have my swords strapped to my back, and I pull out Lux and stare at the moonlight sword in awe and grief.

The nurse sucks in her breath. "Is that real? Weapons aren't..."

Ace comes to my rescue. "We are attending a...how do you say...play of some kind. Forgive us our unusual appearance."

He picks up the paper I dropped and looks at it, then looks at me with an odd expression. "We must be going, don't you think? Wouldn't want to be late to the...play."

I nod, my eyes still unfocused, my heart still beating too loudly against my rib cage. I hear the whoosh of blood in my ears and fight down bile rising in my throat.

When we walk into the cold darkness of Portland's winter night, I suck in a breath. "It was my father. The gargoyle, the guardian...it was my father. His heart. His life given for this sword."

Ace doesn't understand and looks at me in confusion, but I stand still, staring at the blade, at my father's heart. His last gift to me.

Then I look up at Ace, a renewed strength settling into my bones. "Too many have sacrificed so that I can wage this war. It's time to win it."

We leave earth and return to a world of war. A world of conflict. A world of slavery. A world that needs us to save it.

Our forces meet on the river crossing, the sun muted in the sky. The enemy spills over the horizon, thousands of foes under Lucian's command. I do not see the creature, the beast of Darkness. I do not know if this is good or bad. Ace and Dean are somewhere, ordering their soldiers. I haven't seen them in a while, since we split up to better lead our battalions.

Our armies clash on the shallow water. Men fall over each other. Blood sprays into the air. A storm of screams and shouts thunders through the earth. I fly over the battle, past our enemy's front lines. To the hill overlooking the battlefield. Where I will find the opposing generals. Where I will find Lucian.

"The Midnight Star! The Midnight Star has come!" someone cries. A soldier below. Her battalion is the vampires. The ones fighting under Levi and Niam and Asher. A group of them turns and runs. Most stay behind. It matters little. Most of the enemy are Fae, mindless, driven by one purpose. To do as Lucian commands. To win.

I let rage fill me. Rage at what Lucian has done. He robs an entire race of their will and conscience, and now he throws away their lives.

I do not know if what we do is right. This battle. Our side is taking lives as much as theirs. But I know one thing.

When I kill Lucian, the fighting ends.

I grab tighter onto Yami's spikes. "It's time, boy. Now."

He roars and dives down behind the enemy lines. Blue flame erupts from his mouth. We don't target the soldiers. No. We target the earth behind them, creating a wall of fire, cutting Lucian off from his army.

Smoke fills the air. Clouds the sky. I throw my hand in front of my mouth, blocking the vile smog, but some still enters my throat, burning my lungs. I cough and command Yami to fly higher until we find clean air. Below, the battlefield is in chaos. Orange dust hovers over the shore, kicked up by the fighting. Water splashes on the river, red with blood. Blue fire burns beneath the hill. The armies—

Something flies past me.

What—

Again. Something black and sharp.

An arrow. A giant arrow.

I look down to where the commanders would be, and enhance my vision with an incantation. There. In the distance on the hill stand giant contraptions forged from black steel. Ballistae. They fire giant bolts into the air. At us.

"Dodge," I yell, as another one flies toward us.

Yami twirls through the sky, avoiding bolt after bolt.

"We need to get down there. Burn the siege weapons down."

Yami roars, diving at the ballistae. The bolts come faster. One flies above me. One just past my ear.

One—

Yami lurches to the side, flips upside down, and I lose my grip, falling through the sky. I crash down into the earth, onto grass, tumbling to a stop. My legs ache. My hands feel raw. I try to stand and manage. My chest hurts. Maybe a broken rib? If so, it doesn't slow me down much. I run forward searching for Yami. I hear him first. A great big moan. Pain. He's in pain.

Yami. I'm coming. I'm coming boy.

I climb over a hill, and then I see him, lying by the wall of fire, a giant ballista bolt stuck in his wing. Soldiers, one who found their way around the flames, prod at him with spears and swords. He is giant compared to them, like a tiger to mice, but though he snaps and claws at them, he doesn't reach. His movements are small, constrained. It's the bolt, it's hurting him to move. My dragon lies there, near defenseless as people cut at his scales, tear at his wings. I cry out. Feeling his pain as my own.

"Leave him be!" I yell, rushing down the hill.

One of the soldiers looks up at me. "Well, well. There you are."

That voice.

That armor. Red and gold.

He wears the scars from his torture.

Levi stands before me, leading the attack on Yami.

He draws his silver sword. "Remember, girl. I bested you at Stonehill, and I will best you now."

He is the better swordsman, true. But he has my dragon. And no one. No one keeps me from Yami.

I draw Spero and Lux. One blade half white, half black. The other a pale blue, glowing like the moons. Then I close my eyes, recalling the advanced forms Fen taught me. I do not let his memory distract me. There is only the present. Only now.

I open my eyes.

And I charge.

Our blades meet, filling the air with the ringing of steel. Levi is faster than me, parrying blow after blow, but I use my two swords to full advantage, striking twice each time he strikes once. It's the only way I keep up. The only way I keep us tied.

The other soldiers don't enter the fray. I wish they would. Instead, they keep attacking Yami, stabbing at his legs. The dragon whimpers, and I let myself get distracted by his pain.

Levi strikes through my guard, cutting my shoulder. My armor is the only thing that keeps him from taking off my arm. Instead, he gives me a deep cut. I bite down in agony.

Levi hops back, grinning. He could have pressed his advantage, but he gives me a chance to recover. The bastard's enjoying this! He wants to drag out the fight. Wants to hurt me.

I need to end this now. Before a more dangerous enemy like Lucian arrives. Before the soldiers tear Yami apart, causing him to dematerialize.

Every second I waste is a second an innocent Fae or vampire dies in battle.

I need another plan. A better plan. I can't win in a fair fight against Levi. Maybe I could...

"Where is Fenris, I wonder?" asks Levi, prowling around me like a predator. "I would have expected to see him at your side. Did he abandon you, princess? Has Fenris finally run?"

I can't let him get to me. I must focus. Plan. Levi wants to fight me, beat me, humiliate me. I can't let him get reinforcements, but maybe...

Maybe I can get reinforcements of my own.

So I do the hardest thing I can think of. I leave Yami behind.

I turn, running away, running around the wall of fire, toward the armies.

Levi curses behind me. And then he does as I hoped. He follows me.

I sprint as fast as my legs can manage in my heavy armor, my lungs burning with effort. I weave my way through the battlefield, between Fae killing vampires, soldiers fleeing in terror, their morale broken. With an incantation, I enhance my hearing, listening for Levi. His footsteps amongst thousands. I hear him. Drawing closer. Closer. A blade rings through the air.

I turn.

Levi's sword flies at my throat.

He threw it.

I toss up my swords to block.

I'm not fast enough.

His sword rips through the air.

It's almost at my neck.

Something knocks it away.

Dean.

His blade knocks Levi's to the ground. He stands between me and Levi, his black chainmail shimmering in the dim sun. "Get to your dragon," he roars. Then he turns on Levi. The Prince of Envy scrambles, grabbing a sword off the ground, and brother fights against brother.

My plan worked. Dean came to my aid. But now I see the battlefield up close. Corpses upon corpses. Limbs cast to the side. Decapitated faces. My stomach twists and turns, making me sick. I see men and women die before me. People crying for mercy as they bleed out, clutching at their cut open stomachs. And then others die with no passion. They kill mercilessly. The Fae. They are winning.

Lucian is winning.

We need to tip the scales.

We need Zeb's ambush.

But the signal...I can't signal without Yami.

I run, leaving Dean and Levi to fight. I run for Yami. For the soldiers who torture him. They barely see me approach, and I cut them down, not allowing myself to think, to feel sorry. I slaughter them, and when they all lie dead, I pull the bolt from Yami's wing. "Now. The signal!"

Yami opens his mouth, and blue fire erupts into the sky.

I look away from the battlefield, to the forest where Zeb's army hides.

Come on. Come on.

No one comes.

Come on, dammit.

No one comes.

What's happening? Did Zeb betray us?

I wait longer.

No one comes.

I see our army start to break. I see Levi disarm Dean, kicking him down into the sand.

And then, on the hill, I see Lucian.

I see him laugh.

PART II

—Asher—

"What's so funny?" I ask, sitting by my father.

We have a whole tent sent up. Torches on pillars. A nice cozy place with chairs for each of us, me, Lucian, Niam, while a battle rages on below. While innocent people die. This isn't right. Any of it.

We barely even command. Instead of issuing orders, Niam and Lucian eat snacks as we watch, like this is some bloody show, some bloody game.

We only have one guard. A man in golden armor, his entire body covered. Only small slits in his helmet, so you can't even see his eyes. So inhuman. So cold.

Like them. Like me.

No. I must remember why I'm doing this. For Varis. For all Fae.

If I can get a moment alone with Lucian, if I can catch him off guard. I could end this. All of it.

Lucian laughs again. "They just sent their signal," he says, pointing at the blue flames in the sky.

I glance around, studying our backline, our flanks. "Should we be expecting an ambush?"

"We were expecting an ambush, my dear son," says Lucian, chewing on a piece of bread from a platter. "That is why I had spies scouring the landscape. They detected a force traveling from Zeb's lands, so I dispatched the Darkness to dispose of them."

My eyes grow wide. My heart beats faster. "And Zeb?"

The golden guard turns our way at the mention of the prince.

Lucian waves his hand dismissively. "He lives. I told you, I don't wish any of my children to come to harm."

A Fae walks up to me, offering me a platter of grapes and bread. I wave them away, sick at the very thought of food. "Where is he? Where is Zeb?"

Lucian sighs, as if my questions tire him so. "At High Castle, of course. Under guard."

Niam scowls, plopping a grape into his mouth. "He should be executed, if you ask me. Siding with the traitors."

"Now, now," says Lucian. "You've all made mistakes. A father must forgive. He must give chances."

"We're not children anymore," hisses Niam. "He should pay for his actions. So should Dean and Ace."

"There are ways to make things right," says Lucian. "Ways to redeem oneself."

"So," I ask, "is that why your creature is not here? Because it just slaughtered hundreds of vampires?" I try to keep the rage from my tone. I fail.

Lucian nods. "Indeed. It is on its way. But I don't believe we will need it. Even if the tide shifts." He gestures outside the tent, to a huge catapult not far. It isn't with the rest of the army. I'd thought it odd, now I am even more curious.

"One catapult? That will win the battle?"

"It is not the catapult that is important, but the ammunition. See those barrels?"

I do. Hundreds of barrels at the catapult's base.

"Explosives," says Niam, grinning like a fool.

I…"What? Explosives?"

"Yes," says Lucian, casually wiping away bread crumbs with a handkerchief. "If need be, we will fire them at the enemy."

I stand, clenching my fists. "But that will kill everyone. The Fae. The vampires. The Druids are there. Varis."

"I'm sure he we will find a way to survive," says Lucian. "Besides, if he does perish, some other Fae will just gain his powers, and I will control them all the same."

This…this is madness. I need to do something, but I can't, not with Niam here.

Lucian yawns, then motions to the guard. "I grow tired of this fight. Find the girl. Once you capture her, the rest will surrender."

The golden soldier nods, then marches for battle. The earth seems to quake with each of his steps, so heavy is the armor. I've never seen the like.

"Another gift from the Darkness?" I ask, pointing at the soldier.

"In a way," Lucian says, his eyes cold. "In a way."

PART III

—Arianna Spero—

Something comes.

The ground shakes in its wake.

A soldier, larger than any normal man.

Clad in golden armor.

He comes for me.

Yami, now free of the bolt, hisses at the new foe.

The soldier doesn't react. He doesn't fear a dragon. Or perhaps he can't fear. Perhaps he is Fae, doing whatever Lucian wants.

Yami weaves around me protectively, baring his teeth. I raise my swords.

And then we fight.

The soldier is slow, clumsy in movement, using a giant sword as his weapon. I dance around him, slicing past his defenses. But my strikes do nothing against the armor.

Fine. We'll try something else.

I jump back and Yami roars, blasting the soldier with blue flame. He doesn't even try to dodge. The fire hits him, and I raise my hand, shielding my eyes from the overwhelming light. In battles that move so quickly, it seems forever that Yami smothers the enemy with flame. Finally, when he seems too tired to keep breathing fire, he stops, his head dropping, his breath heavy and loud.

I look up. Through the black smoke. Through the burning grass.

Impossible.

The soldier still stands. His armor is scorched, black from the fire, but not melted, not torn apart.

Yami screeches and jumps forward, clawing at the armor. But it won't work.

I try to warn him.

But I'm not fast enough.

Yami's attack does nothing.

The soldier swings his blade down. Down on Yami's neck. And my dragon falls, dematerializing into dust.

No.

How can we win now? How can we win without Yami?

The foe walks forward, his head turning to face me. He has only two slits for eyes, and yet I feel anger in them. A deep rage.

And then I get an idea.

I dash forward, screaming with fervor.

The soldier swings his giant blade, striking for my body.

I leap into the air, over his attack.

And I land on top of him, wrapping my legs around his giant neck. I drop my swords and grab his helmet with my hands. It is hot, burning my fingers, but I ignore the pain, pulling, pulling. I yank the helmet off and throw it to the side.

I jump down, avoiding his strikes, and I grab Spero from the ground.

Then I leap forward.

My blade aimed at his head.

And then I see his face.

His face.

And I can't do it.

I can't end it.

I lower my blade, missing on purpose, and turn to face him.

Before me, clad in scorched armor, his face red with tears, stands Ace.

"Why?" I whisper.

His voice trembles with pain. "Because he wants to lift the curse. Don't you see? He wants to lift the curse. And when he does, I can be with Patricia."

"So for love then," my words are cold. Heartless. They must be. Because if I allow myself to feel, to fully feel, then this betrayal will break me. "I understand," I say. "I do not agree. But I understand."

"I'm sorry," he says.

"I know."

Then he looks past my shoulder. "No!" he yells.

I'm not sure why. Perhaps he changed his mind. Perhaps, though he wished to win, he did not wish to cause me harm. Either way, it doesn't matter. His warning comes too late.

I turn.

And something hits me on the head.

Pain.

Dullness.

Fading.

I collapse.

My consciousness begins to fade.

It's over. I've lost.

Levi stands over me, grinning. He leans down, brushing his lips against my neck. "I believe we were interrupted last time, my princess. But now, I can finish draining your succulent blood."

He bites into me.

And as I fade into darkness, the last thing I see is Ace.

Weeping.

. . .

My feet drag though dust.

Someone is pulling me.

I open my eyes, and my head feels like it's about to explode. Everything is too bright. Too loud.

Men and women shout in the distance. The battle. It feels far off.

The person dragging me let's go, and I fall face first into mud. I push myself up, trying to make out my surroundings. I'm under a canopy, an orange tent. Torches hang on wooden posts, giving off bright light. People sit before me in ornate chairs. Three of them. My vision steadies, and I make them out. Niam. Asher. And Lucian.

Ace walks over to stand by their side. He still wears the fire-kissed armor, but his face is uncovered. It's red, dirty, his hair a brown mess, but he no longer cries.

Levi stands by me. He must have been the one to drag me. I remember what he did, and my hand shoots to my neck. I feel bite marks there, and an ache deep and pulsing.

The Prince of Envy walks forward, addressing the other leaders. "We have her, father."

Lucian doesn't look at his son. Instead he studies the bread in his hand. "Then we have won," he says. "We must let the enemy know we have captured the Midnight Star."

"Allow me," says Levi. "I shall put her head on a spike and parade it through the battlefield."

Lucian puts down the bread, wiping his mouth with fancy handkerchief. "Oh no. Ace will have that honor."

Ace recoils. "I...I..."

Niam and Asher look at him oddly for some reason, like he's not supposed to be here.

Asher. I can't bear to think about him. I look away, forcing my gaze onto Lucian. Thinking of a way to end this.

My swords are gone. Taken.

Or left behind...No. They lie in the corner of the tent. By Ace's feet. He must have carried them.

If I could get to them. If could get to Lux, my moonlight blade, then I have a chance to end this. I can still kill Lucian.

Ace fumbles with his words. "Father, I think it...it—"

"I should have the honor," says Levi, clenching his fists. "I captured her."

Lucian pauses. For the first time, he looks at his son. His face cold. "You? *You?* Please Levi, we all know Ace did all the hard work. Come now, stop wasting time and bring her here."

I expect Levi to explode with fury.

But he drops his head. And instead of seeing the Prince of Envy, I see a little boy. A little boy just trying to please his father.

I remember the story Levi told me. The story of how he used to forge blades, until his father thought him a liar. The story of how Levi, one day, stopped trying to be good.

Broken, beaten, Levi turns to me. He bends down, as if to grab and drag me, but then his hand reaches for his blade.

In a flash, he spins around, throwing his sword at his father.

Lucian grabs it in midair.

He laughs.

"Oh Levi. Finally, you stand up for yourself. And what a pathetic moment it is." He squeezes his hand, and Levi's sword breaks into pieces, falling to the ground.

No one else, not even Niam, seems to enjoy the display. They all look at Levi with a sorrow in their eyes. Even I. For a moment.

Then Lucian rushes forward faster than a blink, and he grabs Levi by the throat. He lifts him into the air, choking the air out of him. "You are worthless," he hisses.

Levi says nothing. But his eyes turn red. And for the first time ever, I see Levi cry.

Lucian tosses him aside like a broken tool, and Levi falls at the outskirts of the tent, clutching at his neck, grasping for breath.

His father retakes his seat, plops a grape into his mouth. "Now, let us return to—"

"You monster!" roars Levi. Trembling, he pushes himself back up. "All I ever wanted was to please you. All I ever wanted was for you to care."

"Then do something!" yells Lucian, spit flying from his mouth. "Do something of worth!"

Levi pauses, and for a moment, there is happiness in his eyes. "Oh, I will father."

Then he grabs a torch off the post.

And throws it at something outside the tent.

A catapult.

Barrels.

And for once, Lucian doesn't laugh at his son. For once, he wears a face of dread.

The torch hits the barrels.

And the hillside explodes.

...

A wave of force hits me, throwing me through the air. I don't know how far I fly, only that it is far. And when I finally land, it is with a deep thud. My chest aches. My leg feels sprained. The world spins around me. I try to calm myself, to make out what is happening.

Dust in the sky, covering the very sun. Ash on my tongue. Fire all around. Debris at my feet. It is chaos. Chaos everywhere.

I stand, despite the pain in my leg, and stumble forward. I need to find my swords. I need them to defeat Lucian. Through the dust, I can no longer tell friend from foe. All I see is people fleeing. And corpses. So many corpses.

Their bodies charred.

Like Daison.

Fear grips me. Consumes me. I have failed. Our army is broken, gone. Even if I defeat Lucian, who is there left to save?

I do not know.

I do not know who yet lives.

Dean?

I saw Levi disarm him. Did he finish the job?

What of Varis? Did he fall in battle?

I don't know. I don't know. I don't know.

I can no longer walk. It's too hard. Too hard to keep going. I need to rest. Yes. Rest. I find a stone on the sand. A nice place to sit. To sit and close my eyes and rest.

Yes. This feels good.

I can just dream.

Dream of another time. A time that feels so long ago. When Fen first brought me to Stonehill. He showed me his favorite part of the castle. The great tree that grows through the center of the grand hall. *"I know it's not what people expect when they hear Prince of War, but—"* He grinned at me. Guilelessly. Beautifully. Like we shared a secret. He gave me a ring. And I remember thinking, no matter what happens, I will always be grateful for Fenris Vane.

A voice pulls me from my stupor.

"You can't run, Princess." Niam. He walks out from the dust, his white cape trailing behind him, a silver sword in his hand.

Not just any sword. My sword. Lux. He must have picked it up somewhere after the explosion.

"Ace couldn't kill you, that was clear," he says. "But I will not make the same mistake." He stands over me, places my own sword against my throat.

How fitting.

Light will be my end.

Because Darkness has won.

I close my eyes. Falling back into the dream. It feels so real. Me and Fen and Baron together. I even hear the howl.

"You really *should* stop getting kidnapped."

His voice.

So close.

It can't be...

I open my eyes.

And see him.

He stands before me.

He came back.

"Fen."

PART IV

—Fenris Vane—

I step in front of Arianna, protecting her with my body. I should have returned sooner. She is barely conscious now. So weak. But I cannot focus on my mistakes. I must focus on how to right them.

"You will not touch her," I say, raising my blade, Baron growling at my side.

Niam shakes his head. "Remember what I told you, brother. Next time we saw each other—"

"You'd force me into submission?" I laugh. "I doubt it."

That gets to him. He charges in a blind rage. A mistake. One should never let emotion dictate strategy.

I parry his strike and jump behind him. He turns to follow me, lashing out furiously. But he has already lost.

Baron jumps on his back, tearing into his shoulder.

Niam falls, screaming, limbs flailing.

He drops his sword, and I kick it away. No. It's Arianna's sword. How—

Something growls in the distance.

A deep raw sound. It chills to the bone.

The dust in the air begins to change. It grows darker. Black as night.

It's here.

The Darkness.

The creature.

I hear a whimper. Baron!

Niam grabs the wolf by the neck and twists. A crack. Baron's neck snaps.

And he dematerializes, fading into white dust.

Niam stands, grinning, seemingly unaffected by his bloody shoulder. He looks into the dark clouds of dust, to the growl that grows louder, and he laughs like a madman. "You cannot win, Fenris. You cannot defeat the Darkness."

"It's not my duty to fight the Darkness," I say. "It's hers."

He frowns, then his eyes follow mine. To Arianna.

She stands, grabbing her sword from the ground. Her eyes meet mine. "You're here," she says.

"I was always here." Even when I thought to leave, my heart, my mind, it stayed with her.

She nods. And turns to face the Darkness.

The creature emerges from the shadows, shaking the ground with its massive form. Its black fur slithers and coils like snakes. Its face twists and turns in grotesque images of half man and half beast. Sharp teeth protrude from its gaping maw, an endless pit of black.

The creature roars, and it's as if the whole world threatens to unravel in its wake.

Arianna doesn't flinch.

She steps forward, moving on air, gliding on shadows.

Somehow, she is flying.

The power of the Midnight Star. She and Yami are one.

I see it in her eyes. The colors of midnight. I see it on her skin. It shimmers like stars.

What the dragon can do, she can do, I realize. They were never separate. Not really.

Then Arianna, the Midnight Star, streaks across the sky, a moonlight blade in hand, and she fights the Darkness.

PART V

—Ace—

I wake to silence. Shadows all around me. My memories return in pieces.

Levi. The explosion.

I push myself to stand.

Somehow, I survived. Probably because of this bloody armor. I should have never created it. I should have never used it.

Why did I fight for Lucian?

For Patricia?

For love?

If she could see this, if she could know the chaos I caused, she would not dare look at me.

I betrayed her. I betrayed myself.

I stand amongst the rubble. Amongst the piles of corpses. And I make my way back to the tent. Back to what's left anyway.

There, on the hill, I find him.

He lies with his face in the mud, his body black and charred. Still. Lifeless.

Gently, I turn him over. His silver hair has burned away, but his face remains. Oh, Levi...

He did cruel things, but right now, all I can remember is the little boy who stood up for his brother, who defended his inventions while others called them silly. For a while, I stay there, back in the Silver Gardens, back when it was just me and Levi, playing together with a new toy I made. That is how I will always remember him. Happy. Innocent. Before the world turned him into a monster.

I kiss his forehead.

And then I go to find father.

It's time he paid for what he did.

PART VI

—Fenris Vane—

The Midnight Star fights the Darkness, and I fight Niam. It should be easy. He's injured, his shoulder torn open and raw. He has a sword, some random one he found one the ground, nothing special. But...

Something is wrong.

Every time Arianna and the creature clash, I feel a thud in my mind, like a hammer trying to break open my skull. Images flash before my mind. Images I've tried to forget.

The Grey Mountain.

Me climbing to the peak.

A storm.

I seek shelter in a cave.

And then…

Then I see something new.

This didn't happen…this couldn't happen…

I see Marasphyr in the cave. Together we wait out the storm. We grow close. She promises to help me slay the Grey Beast.

Together, we travel higher up. We face the creature. A giant thing of black bones. It tears into me.

I almost die.

I see something. A vision. A vision of my mother. She is Fae. I am Fae.

I awaken. Stronger than before.

I leap through the sky and slay the beast with one blow.

Then Marasphyr sees me for what I am. She guesses at my past. I learn about the lies. The secrets. I was always Fae. The vampires killed my mother.

I want revenge. I need it. I keep my new revelations secret from my brothers as I plan. Together, Marasphyr and I start a rebellion. One other joins our ranks.

A traveler.

Tavian Gray.

Something...something pierces my belly. The memories fade, only for a moment, and I see Niam before me, smiling. His sword sticks out of my gut. I don't feel the pain. I'm already fading, back into my memories.

"I told you brother," says Niam. "This time, you submit."

He drives the blade deeper into my belly.

Now pain grips me.

Blood pours from my mouth.

I'm dying, I realize. But...

I've died before.

Once, I awoke to Asher, and he told me the truth. He told me I was a Druid. But I had died before. When I died on Grey Mountain, I awoke knowing I was Fae. But somehow, I forgot.

Time to remember.

I fall back and fade into the abyss once more.

...

I walk on a land with no earth and sky.

Baron at my side.

He nudges me forward.

I already know what I will see.

Before me, my mother.

Her hair long and wild.

Her voice a soft melody.

She stands aside.

And then I see him.

Father?

No. It's not my father I see.

It's me. I wear a green cloak, my ears are long. And in my hand, I hold a pale blue sword. A moonlight blade.

I was...

I am...

The Moonlight Prince.

...

I do not know how long I sleep before I wake. But it seems not long. Niam walks away, toward Arianna and the creature. He will join the battle, he will help the Darkness win.

I try to stand, to help, but I feel woozy, tired. My vision spins.

Someone emerges from the shadows. I know her. Marasphyr.

"What are you doing here—"

"Shh," she says, putting a finger to her lips, her voice smooth and light. "I felt it too. The breaking of the curse. It weakens every time Arianna hurts the beast."

I try to make sense of her words. "Curse? What curse?"

"You don't remember yet? You don't remember what we did?" She starts to pace, shadow drifting behind her. It moves unnaturally, following her steps. Something familiar, this.

"Very well, Fenris, I will tell you," she says, sitting down by my side. "I've wished to tell you for a long time."

"What do you mean?"

She looks at me. Her eyes dark pools, something sinister swirling within them. "You believe you met me at the Black Lotus. But this is not true. We met before. On Grey Mountain."

"Yes," I say, the memories returning. "You helped me fight the beast."

She smiles. "Yes. I did. And we fell in love. That I am certain of." She pauses. "During the battle, you almost died. When you awoke, you...you were Fae. You were always Fae. You didn't understand at first, but slowly you gained information. A clever question there, an observation here. You realized what had happened. You learned of Avakiri. And you wanted revenge. For your people. For all Fae. You wanted them free.

"So you contacted me. Together we began a rebellion, drawing Outlanders to our cause, even some of the Four Tribes. Our greatest asset was Tavian Gray. An ancient Fae, older than the Unraveling. Many trusted him, admired him, and he recruited them. Soon, we had an army. A small one, but an army.

"We fought a war of attrition. Attacking a caravan here. A shipment there. You kept your true identity secret from the Fae, always covering your face to all but me and Tavian, and you kept your revelations secret from your brothers. That way, you could still be Prince of War, could still attend the council meetings. You gathered information on defenses, resources, and you used it to our advantage.

"At one point, we managed to steal an old Fae relic. A moonlight sword. It became your blade. And it wasn't long until the rebels, until we all, began calling you the Moonlight Prince. You were our symbol, Fenris, our symbol of hope. You weren't a High Fae. The High Fae had failed us, we didn't want another one. Not really. You...you were something more. A man from legend...like the Primal One himself. You had come to free us.

"But it was not enough. Our attacks only made them strengthen their defenses. Soon we began losing battles, loosing soldiers. Our numbers dwindled. Our supporters began to flee. And so we devised a plan.

"Tavian, you, and I, would perform a ritual. We would summon a power long lost, and with it we would defeat the vampires."

Realization shatters me. My hands tremble with sorrow. This…all that has transpired recently…this is my fault. "We…" I can barely bring myself to say it. But I must. The memories return and I must face them. "We summoned the Darkness."

"Yes," says Marasphyr. "And we could not control it. The Darkness attacked our own, spreading through Avakiri. It killed innocent men, women, and children. It killed Tavian's family. Us three however, it did not kill. Through the ritual, we had developed some kind of bond with it, gained some of the powers we had wished to summon. But, upon seeing the carnage, you attacked the beast. Your moonlight sword, a blade of legend, could harm it, and somehow, somehow you trapped the Darkness. I did not see the final battle, but Tavian and I arrived at the end. It is then, as you locked the Darkness away, that it cursed us three.

"Tavian, it cursed to never forget. So that he may live with the memory of his wife and child dying every single day. Me, it cursed to remember the future, but never to change it. To see horrible things and never stop them. And you, Fenris, you it cursed to forget your true self. To forget me and Tavian, the people you loved. So that once again you had to live a lie.

"And so you returned to being Fenris Vane, Prince of War. I sought you out, found you at the Black Lotus. I tried to tell you the truth, but you could never hear me. You could never remember the time we shared, or the person you truly were. I tried rekindling our relationship, but it was never the same. You were never the same."

I study her, memories of our time together returning. They seem a past life. We could have lived a good life together, perhaps. But now it will never be. "You..." I say, watching the shadows swirl around her. "You said the Darkness bonded with us..."

"Yes."

"Gave us powers..."

"Yes."

"You...You are the Wraith."

She smiles. And for a second her entire body turns to shadow, to Darkness. And then she is back, Marasphyr, with her pale skin and black hair. "Yes. I am the one you call the Wraith. After we were cursed, Tavian sought to conceal his powers, to deny them, while you could not remember your own. I, however, I studied them. Fed them. Grew in power. So, yes it was me in the cave. The people sacrificed themselves to give me power. But, I did not ask them to. I know I said I did, but I was trying to scare you. They performed a ritual, a ritual much like we did, and it summoned me, gave me strength. I did not wish for it to happen." She looks down, but I cannot tell if she is truly sad or just remembering. "I asked you to bring me Tavian Gray because

I missed him. We had parted on poor terms when he learned I had kept using my new abilities. But he was one of the few people who knew my true self, knew my secrets. I wanted reconciliation. You, of course, failed to bring me Tavian right away, but you did eventually, unknowingly. We talked. He still hates me. Hates what I am. But at least for a while, we talked."

I see sorrow in her. Regret.

"You can still do right," I say. "Help me defeat the Darkness. Help me save Arianna."

She wipes her eyes. A single tear. "I see, even with your memories restored, you still love her. I suppose I knew it would be so. I…" She pauses, leaving something unsaid, then caresses my face. "Goodbye, Fenris Vane. I do not think we shall see each other again. This world has been too painful for me. There are many others. And perhaps in one of them I will find happiness."

She leans down and gently kisses my forehead, and then opens the palm of my hand and places something in it—a ring. Arianna's ring. "I was asked to give this to you." And then she stands, walking away.

"Wait," I plead. "Stay. Help me fight."

She looks back, smiling. "Oh Fenris, you don't need my help. You beat the Darkness before, remember?"

And then with a wink, she vanishes into shadow.

I beat the Darkness, she said. I beat the Darkness. And I will do so again.

I stand, dust flying off my body, and slip Arianna's ring onto my little finger. Niam notices me, his eyes going wide. "How are you alive?"

I ignore him, running for Arianna and the creature. I don't bother finding my sword. I won't need it. Not against the beast.

I know what I must do.

"Find Lucian!" I yell to Arianna. "I will fight the creature. When I kill it, Lucian will be weak, vulnerable." Because he is bound to the Darkness just like I am bound. It is why I felt weak every time Arianna hurt the Darkness. It is why Lucian will be weak when I kill the beast. And it is why, I realize, I have escaped death so many times.

"Are you sure?" asks Arianna, weaving through the sky, her blade clashing against the creature's claws.

"Yes. Now go."

She nods. And like the wind she flies, disappearing into the black dust.

The creature looks at me. And then it speaks. "I...I remember you..." it says with a hundred voices. "You... you summoned me."

"I did. And now I will send you back."

The Darkness laughs. A chuckle that shakes the very earth. "You have no moonlight blade."

Yes. But I know where to find one, because I remember where I left it.

Tavian said Fae had scoured the lands searching for the moonlight sword after the prince fought the Darkness, but they never found it. They never found it because it was locked away. Locked away within the creature.

I run forward, the earth rising below my feet, creating a hill as I move, pushing me up into the sky. I have never used such power before, but it comes easily now. Because I know who I am. Who I truly am.

I look to my side, and I see Baron there, running with me.

It's just you and me boy. One last time.

Perhaps I imagine it, but he seems to smile.

Then the earth pushes us forward, and we fly into the air. Over the beast. It claws at us, but moves too slowly. And up here, in the sky. I see it. The moonlight sword. Just where I left it.

Lodged in the creature's back.

I fall, Baron at my side, and together we land on the giant beast's neck. I grab onto its thick, coiling hair, holding myself from falling. Baron grabs on with his teeth.

The beast flails about, trying to reach us, but it cannot, for its arms are not long enough, and if it turns, we turn with it, holding onto its mane.

I jump to the side.

To the blade.

A giant thing of pale blue steel, covered with intricate carvings of the Fae. I grab the handle with both hands. And for the Fae I failed when I summoned this creature, for the Fae I failed when I allowed slavery to continue, for my own people, I drive the blade deeper. I drive it into the creature's heart.

And I kill the Darkness.

PART VII

—Ace—

I find my father at the very top of the hill. One moment, he is smiling, overlooking the battlefield cloaked in shadow. And the next, he yells out in pain, falling to his knees. He clutches his heart. "Something, something is wrong," he whispers.

I do not know what happened. I don't care.

He deserves pain.

A gust of wind hits me, and I see the darkness is fading below. The shadow that had covered the smoke withdraws. And from the remnants, emerges Arianna.

She flies through the sky and lands before us.

For a moment, she glances my way, and an understanding passes between us. Then she turns to my father. Raising her blade. Lux, I believe she called it. Light.

When Arianna speaks, her voice is soft, and yet it echoes with a power unimaginable. "Once, you were king of these lands. You were tasked with protecting your people. You were tasked with bringing peace." She steps forward, any trace of fear gone from her face. All weakness and pain gone. "But you lost your way." She gestures to the battlefield below, to the mountains of corpses. "This is not why you were chosen. This is not your duty. You have failed yourself. You..."

Lucian stumbles back.

"Are..."

He looks to me, eyes pleading for help.

"Not..."

He reaches out to me.

"Worthy."

"Please..." whispers my father.

I do not help him. For Levi. For the Fae.

"This land," says Arianna. "This land belongs to no one." She slashes her sword through the air, and the blade known as Light cuts the vampire king's throat.

He collapses, his life bleeding out of him, his eyes losing focus. One final time, he raises his hand in the air, and he whispers. "I only wanted...I only wanted to see home again."

And the great king dies.

And the war ends.

PART VIII

—Asher—

The shadow retreats. The dust settles.

The explosion Levi caused tossed me far down the hill, into the shallow waters. There I lay, my limbs and chest full of pain. I lay until the fighting stopped. I lay until the sun came up. Then, with my remaining strength, I pushed myself to stand, to search for the thing one I hold dearest.

I find him in the sky, battling a prince in white.

Varis meets my gaze. His eyes are no longer glazed over. His eyes are his own. And in them, I see love.

Niam turns to face me, his white cloak drifting in the wind, his sword in hand. His shoulder is torn open. His leg is cut and nearly immobile. He can barely stand. "So what will it be brother? Vampire or Fae? Who do you side with?"

I find a spear on the ground and hold the weapon tight. Tears well in my eyes. "It was never about race, brother. Not for me. It was always about people. Just people. And what makes them who they are."

Then I charge forward. And ram the spear through my brother's heart.

We collapse together. Him bleeding, his eyes blank. Me clutching his lifeless body, weeping against his chest.

I do not know how long I hold him. My brother. My kin.

Someone touches my shoulder.

I turn and see him.

His face kind.

His voice soft.

Varis.

"It's alright," he says. "It's alright, my love." And then he takes me into his arms and holds me close.

I speak through sobs. "I failed you. I failed the Fae. I didn't bring peace. Only death. Only more death."

"No, Asher." He caresses my head gently. "You could never fail me. Whatever you do, whoever you become, you will always be my Karasi. The Spirit of my heart."

PART IX

—Kayla Windhelm—

When we arrive at the battlefield, the war is already over, but the work is not yet done. Tavian and I gather up the survivors and begin efforts to tend to the wounded. There are hundreds of them. Thousands.

We should have been here, I think. We should have stopped this.

But in the end, what would we have done? The battle is won. There were always going to be casualties.

But I can do better next time. Next time, I can prevent wars in the first place. I could be a leader. A Druid.

"You are good at this," says Tavian as we scour the battlefield for more injured. It wasn't long after Arianna left the Rift, and then Fen, that we realized we had to return as well.

"Good at what?" I ask, rolling over bodies, checking for life.

"At serving others."

I chuckle. "I thought you'd say leadership, or command."

He smiles. "I did. For isn't that what serving others is?" He winks at me, and we continue on.

"Will you leave again?" I ask. "To avoid politics?"

"No," he says, wrapping his arm around me. "Now that the Darkness is defeated, I feel the curse retreating. I feel my memories fade. I will remember my wife's face and the faces of my children, I think. Yes. I think I would like that. But the rest I will forget. And then I will finally have peace."

"And what will you do with this peace?" I ask.

He pulls me closer, pushing his lips against mine. "I will share it. Share it with the woman I love." We kiss again, Riku chirping on my shoulder. The moment is perfect. Timeless.

And then a scream breaks it.

I rush forward, looking for the injured.

And then I find her, lying in the dirt, her leg severed at the knee, a spear sticking out from her gut. She wears blue robes, and a serpent coils around her arm.

"We must put pressure on her leg," I say, falling to her side.

"No," whispers Metsi. "No, please. I am tired of this world. I want to rest. Yes. Rest."

"You can rest later, I promise," I say, ripping off a piece of my dress and wrapping it around her leg.

Metsi chuckles. "I thought you would hate me. I was your enemy. Your foe."

"But right now, you are someone who needs help."

"Yes. Yes. I do." She gazes into my eyes. "End it. Please."

My hands start to shake. My stomach twists. "I...I can't..."

"Too long have I walked this earth. Too long have I been a Keeper. It is time for someone else. Someone worthy."

I force myself to smile for her. "But you are worth—"

"No. Do not lie to me. Not now. I failed my people. I failed myself. I accept that. I embrace it. It is the only way to learn. And my learning is not yet finished. No. There is a world beyond. A place where my family waits for me. I long to be with them. Please..."

I pull back, my eyes burning. "I...I..."

Tavian grabs my shoulder. "Let me," he says. "I know what it is like to live a life of pain. I do not wish it upon anyone." He steps in front of me and draws a dagger from his belt. "I will make it quick."

Metsi smiles, looking to the sky. "Thank you. Thank you..."

And then Tavian bends down, and Metsi, Keeper of Wadu, dies.

Something leaves her body. Something pure and ethereal. Into the clouds it disappears, searching, searching for one who is worthy.

15

AND SO IT BEGINS

"No matter what happens, I will always be grateful for Fenris Vane."

— Arianna Spero—

The sun is out, and I've never been so glad to feel the heat of it on my skin. I sit by the creek, letting my bare feet dip into the cool water as the sun warms my legs and arms and dries me. After the battle, I couldn't stop shaking, and I had to get the blood and dirt and sweat and grime off of me. I had to be alone. I had to breathe and think and process.

It's over.

It's truly over.

We won.

The Fae are no longer mentally enslaved.

But the cost was high. We lost so many.

Fen and Asher and Dean and Zeb...they lost their brothers. Brothers who maybe deserved their fate in my eyes, but brothers who had been together for longer than I can conceive. The realms lost their leaders. They lost their father. Everything is changing, and change often hurts, even when it's good for us.

There will be pain. But there can now also be healing.

I kick at the water, splashing with my foot just to see the light reflect on it. Light has returned. The Darkness has been vanquished.

My hair is nearly dry and so is the simple tunic I wore under my armor and rinsed off in the creek. I slip it over my naked body and resume my spot.

Yami is asleep on the rock next to me, nearly purring in contentment. I rest a hand over my belly, imagining the life that still grows within. It's a girl, I think. And she is strong. She has already survived so much.

It's so still, so peaceful, that I hear his footsteps before he reaches me.

"I wondered if you'd come," I say. I turn to face him, this man who is everything to me. And I know what I must do. It will break me, but it will save him.

He crouches before me and I place a hand on his stubbled face. "I love you," I tell him. "Thank you for coming back. For helping with the fight."

He starts to speak, but I put a finger over his mouth. I need to finish this now, or I'll never be able to. "Back in the Rift, I left you so I could do what I had to do. What

I knew in my heart was right. It hurt beyond words, but I had to choose myself, even over you." I suck in my breath and will my eyes to stay dry just a little bit longer. "Today, I realized I have to leave you for you. Because I love you more than anything. Because I want you to be happy, even more than I want you with me. I have to stay here. I have to try to be a leader to these people, whatever that looks like. I have to help in whatever way I can. It's my calling. My destiny. My choice. It's the only way I can authentically live my life without regret. But you...you don't have to do that. You don't have to walk the same path. I've been thinking a lot about what you said to me in the Rift, about how long you've been living under this curse, under these expectations. How Lucian and your brothers and this world forced you into a mold that never gave you any other choices. I'm not going to do that to you. So, Fen, my love, my heart...I release you." My voice chokes, but I continue, because if I stop, if I pause, I'll never get through this. And I must. For him. "I release you from any agenda I may have had for you and your future. I release you from any obligation you've had to this world, to these people. Even to me and to our child. I release you because I love you and I want you to be free to choose your own path. It's the only way to be happy. You can't live your life trying to make someone else happy. You can't live your life for me. You have to live it for you."

The tears are falling when I finish my speech, but I no longer care. I got it out, all the words I knew I'd have to say. The hardest words I've ever said. Part of me wants to take them all back, suck the words in and pretend they were never spoken, and instead beg him to stay, to be with me, to rule with me. But I can't. I won't. To love someone, to truly love them, is to love them without expectation or agenda. To love someone is to let them be free.

A silence hangs heavy between us. Even Yami and Baron are both still, silent, though Yami woke sometime during this talk.

When I look at Fen, my chest clenches in longing and pain. Every line on his face is as familiar as my own. His eyes, those piercing blue orbs, pull me in and I want to swim in them forever. His arms, his chest, I want nothing more than to be held by him and for him to never let me go.

But I can do this. If I have learned nothing else over the past several months since my mother lapsed into a coma, it's that I am much stronger than I ever imagined. I have been tested time and again, pushed to every limit I have, physically, mentally and emotionally. I have endured imprisonment, torture, a death sentence and war. I have learned and grown and found magic and strength within.

And so I can do this.

I can let the man I love lead a life of peace.

Without me.

My hand falls to my stomach again.

Without us.

Fen pulls away from me and I drop my head so he doesn't see how hard this is.

"Arianna?"

His voice is deep, raw, powerful.

I look up and he's on his knees, holding a ring. The ring he first gave me what feels like a lifetime ago. The ring I left with Marasphyr to give to him when I left the Rift. I admit I was skeptical she'd actually do it.

"Marry me," he says. "Be my wife. My partner. My Queen."

My heart skips and there's a whooshing sound in my ears that I assume is my blood doing some kind of primal dance in my head. "What? But..."

"I heard what you said. I listened to you, now I need you to listen to me," he says. "I was wrong. About this world, about our people...about myself. I'd forgotten who I was. But I remember now. I know who I am. I have found my purpose. And it is with you."

I'm about to interrupt him, to point out that he can't become king just to be with me, but he places a finger over my lips.

"Let me finish."

I nod, and he brushes his hand against my cheek before continuing. "I was under a curse, but not the one

I thought." He tells me of the Darkness, of what he and Tavian and Marasphyr did so many years ago. He tells me of their curses, and how it affected each of them differently. "When the Darkness weakened, it also created cracks in my curse. Memories began filtering in, and I started to remember who I was. Who I truly was. I was the Moonlight Prince. It was my sword that was originally lost. With it, I could help you destroy the Darkness. I could undo the damage I'd done. And once the curse was completely broken, I felt all the parts of myself returning. I don't just want you, Arianna, though the gods know I've never wanted anything so badly as I do you—but I want this too." He holds up his hands and gestures to everything around us. "I want to bring peace to the Fae and vampires. I want to help you create a new kind of government, a new life for our people. I want to raise our child in a world that we help make better. I want to be king. I'm not running away anymore. I'm not Lucian's son, I'm the son of the two women who loved me enough to give up everything for me. My Fae mother died bringing me into the world, and my vampire mother gave me her own blood to save me. I am not made of war, but of love, and I want to bring that love to my wife, my child, and my kingdom. Both of our kingdoms."

My hands are trembling and more tears are flowing down my face. Both Yami and Baron are sitting at attention, ears perked, watching us raptly.

"Say yes," he begs, his eyes so earnest it nearly destroys me.

"Yes," I say, my throat clogged with emotion. "Yes, I'll marry you, Fenris Vane, my Moonlight Prince."

He slips the ring onto my finger and pulls me against him. The day is fading, and as the sun sets and the moons rise in the sky, I revel in the joy my heart feels at knowing I get to be with this man forever.

"Marry me now," he says after a long silence of holding each other.

"Now?"

"Yes, now, here. We can break the curse tonight. Free your mother. Begin our lives. Unless you have a burning urge to finish out your months with my brothers? Ace perhaps? Or Zeb?"

I choke out a laugh. "No, I'm good. Thanks, though. But, don't we need someone to officiate, or paperwork or something?"

He shakes his head. "Not in this world. Yami and Baron are powerful Spirits, and can bear witness. We can speak our vows in their presence. We can have the big ceremony if you want, later, but tonight, right now, I want to know you are mine forever."

And so we stand and hold each other's hands. Yami and Baron take their roles very seriously and give the short ceremony full attention.

"I take you, Arianna Spero, to be my wife, my partner, my lover, my Queen, for now and all eternity. Not
even death can sever this vow or my love for you."

His words spark a glow in my chest that makes my
whole body feel on fire. "And I take you, Fenris Vane,
to be my husband, my partner, my lover, my King, for
now and all eternity. Not even death can sever this vow
or my love for you."

When he kisses me, I feel a magic move through us,
slowly tearing apart at the contract I signed. Yami and
Baron seem to sense a shift in the mood around us and
disappear into the forest as Fen lays me down on a thick
bed of grass.

He leans over me, his long, hard body pressed
against mine. "You're my wife now. Forever and always."

"Forever isn't long enough," I whisper. "But it's a
start."

There are no more words. Not for a very long time.
This isn't like the first time, the wine induced coupling
that led to our child's conception. It's not even like
the second time, the frantic lovemaking inspired by a
world out of time. This time, it is us, fully present and
together, fully committed and in full memory of who we
are and what we want in this life.

It is more than sex. More than physical need and
desire. It is loosing myself in the pure joy of this bond

I share with a man I can now call my husband. It is the connection of our skin, the rapid fire of nerve endings as our hands explore each other, the incredible and indescribable feeling of being one with someone my soul is so bonded to. I loose myself in him. In us. In our joining. In our oneness.

For those hours of exploration and love making, we are the only two people in the universe. Nothing else exists. Nothing else matters. I am completely absorbed by the love I have for this man, and I can see the love he has for me in his eyes. I've never seen him more at peace. More happy. More alive.

When we are spent, our legs draped over each other's, my arm reaching over his broad chest and his arms wrapped around me, I sigh deeply, content at last.

In letting him go, I have found him again.

"There's one more part of the contract we must fulfill before my mother will be free," I whisper against his chest.

I can hear his heart beat accelerate. "We can do that later."

I look up at him, into his eyes. "I'm not afraid. You're not a monster. It doesn't have to be a curse."

He blinks slowly, letting my words sink in. Then he nods and adjusts our bodies so that he's leaning over me again. "Are you sure, Arianna? There's no going back from this."

I pause, my hand falling to the gentle curve of my stomach. "Will it hurt our baby?" I don't want to wait, but I will for her.

"No. Our child is already part vampire and will not be hurt. But you need to be sure…for yourself."

"I'm sure. I'm ready to take the Blood Oath. I'm ready to become one of you. And with us both carrying the blood of the Fae and vampire, we can be a unified force of unity for all of our people."

He nods, and I sit up. "What do we need to do?"

"It's a blood exchange." He bites his wrist and holds it to my mouth.

I place my lips against the blood and feel a sharp prick against my neck.

And then it begins.

EPILOGUE

"I love you, Arianna Spero. I love you."

—Fenris Vane—

I shouldn't be this nervous.

But still, here I am, shaking in my silk and satin white dress, like a fall leaf about to face winter.

I'm surrounded by opulence, in a dressing room the size of a large apartment. Carved wood accented with silver and gold furniture create an elegant, warm vibe, and everywhere there are flowers in full bloom. Yami is sniffing a bouquet recently brought in, his eyes closed as he inhales deeply.

I haven't seen Fen since this morning after our hunt. Being a vampire has taken some getting used to, but now...now I relish the moments running free in the woods with my husband. Shortly after we were both whisked away for matters of state, and planning.

I can handle the politics. The party planning is another story.

This is the first moment I've had alone in the last six hours, and I decide to follow Yami's lead and breathe in the smell of fresh flowers.

It's stunning to me that it's already been a year since the night Fen and I said our vows under the starry sky beside the river. This is our anniversary, but it's also so much more.

It's the day we celebrate with family, friends, and our kingdoms.

It's the day we come together in the eyes of all who know us.

I'm lost in thought when the door to my room cracks open, and Kayla walks in. "They're here," she says with a grin.

My pulse quickens in excitement. "Bring them in, please."

Kayla is dressed in stunning layers of gold and silver and looks as much like a bride as I do. I'm determined to follow the human tradition of tossing the bouquet, and I'm totally going to cheat and use magic to make sure Kayla catches it. She and Tavian are next in line for this particular dance, if that sparkly ring on her finger is any indication.

Kayla smiles at me and her phoenix preens on her shoulder. "You look beautiful. But you're missing something."

She sets down a golden box and opens the lid. "A proper queen needs a proper crown. One of her very own."

My eyes fill with tears when I see it. It's stunning. Gorgeous. It's gold and silver, inlaid with gems that sparkle in the firelight. The design has an elemental feel to it. And in the center is a stone that glows with a soft silver light. A light I've seen before.

"I harvested the metal and gems from both Inferna and Avakiri, and for the center stone..."

"You used the guardian's heart. The moonlight steel." My father's heart.

She nods. "I thought it fitting, and that he would approve. You have done the impossible. You have defeated the Darkness that ensnared this world, and you have brought peace between the vampire, Fae and Shade. You are the unifying force of our world. He gave his heart because he saw into yours, and it was worthy. It always has been."

Now the tears are flowing, damn it all.

She takes the crown from me and places it on my head, securing it with ribbon and pins, then leaves me alone with my thoughts and my dragon.

I turn and look in the mirror. The mirror I fought to have in all the realms. Travel is now allowed. Mirrors are no longer banished.

My sparkling midnight hair is pulled into a myriad of braids and woven together with silver ribbon. My eyes are lined with dark kohl, making the green pop. My lips are stained dark berry. And my dress is beaded with rhinestones and pearls.

I look like a bride.

I look like a Queen.

The peace Kayla speaks of is still in its infant stage. There is still unrest in many parts of Inferna and Avakiri. There is still infighting, prejudice, hate. Lifetimes of segregation and war will not end in a year. Or even many years. But we've made a start. We've reshaped the government of Inferna. Made slavery illegal in all realms. Made non-consensual feeding illegal. Created a new commerce and labor structure to support fair compensation and at will employment. It required a lot of reading and studying and bringing non-technical ideas from my world to this one to see how we might do things differently. And it's still a work in progress. I'm new to this. So is Fen. But we have surrounded ourselves with wise counsel from both the vampire and Fae, and we work daily to make sure every voice is heard.

I turn when I hear the door open and throw myself into the arms of the two people standing there.

Es and Pete wear smiles as big as mine as we hug.

"Girl, you look ah-mazing!" Es says in her southern way.

Pete nods. "Never looked better, Princess. Or should I say Queen?"

"You can just say Ari." I hold each of their hands, afraid if I let go they'll disappear. "I'm so glad you could come. I've missed you both so much."

"We wouldn't miss this for anything," Es says. "Besides, Pete's been dying to see Varis again and pick his brain. That poor Fae is going to be begging us to go back to our own world by the time this celebration is over."

I laugh at that. "I'm sure Varis will be excited to have his most enthusiastic pupil back. Fen and I are so busy, he has to practically kidnap us to continue our training. And there always seems so much to learn, even after all this time."

Es looks around the room, then frowns. "Where is she? Where is my godchild?"

"Ah, your true motives have been revealed. You came for the baby above all. Confess."

"I came for all of you. But yes, that little one is high on my list."

As if on cue, the door opens again, and Es screeches.

"The little angel has arrived," I say, my heart growing bigger every time I lay eyes on my child. She's dressed in gold and silver, with a bow on her head. Her eyes are blue with green flecks, and she's the most amazing thing I've ever seen.

And seeing my mother holding her—that makes everything I've endured to get here worth it. My mother, who no longer limps, who no longer suffers any pain, who chose to stay on this world to be closer to us and help with her granddaughter...it's all too perfect. My heart can hardly hold the joy I feel right now.

I take the baby from her and Kayla tsks from behind everyone. "Careful she doesn't spit up and ruin your dress before the ceremony."

"Oh hush," I chide, as my mom slips a cloth over my shoulder. "Es, Pete, this is Princess Aya'zee, my daughter. Aya'zee, these are two of your godparents."

I hand the baby over to Es and she coos over the infant with big smiles. "What does her name mean?"

"It's a variation of the word peace in ancient Fae," Kayla says, answering for me.

There's a knock on the door and Asher pokes his head in. "It's time, my Queen."

"You look dashing as always," I tell the prince.

He preens and winks. "Of course I do. Would you expect anything less?"

I grin and kiss Aya'zee on the head. "Let's do this."

The throne room is packed with Fae and vampire nobility from Inferna and Avakiri. There was a lot of argument about whether to have the ceremony in High Castle or Avakiri, but the ruined palace of my Fae lineage is still under repair, so we scrapped both ideas and chose Stonehill. The room is lit by magic, with lights of gold and silver shooting over our heads like falling stars. It's standing room only as I walk to the door and wait.

I will not be walked down the aisle by my father, nor my mother. I will not be given away like a prize or possession.

Instead, Fen and I decided we'd walk the aisle together. As one.

And so he joins me, and his eyes light up when he sees me. A grin spreads over his face as he approaches. "My wife. My love. You look beautiful."

"Why thank you, my prince."

As we walk down the aisle, I take note of all the familiar faces here to support us. Kal'Hallen, Fen's Keeper. Baldar, the potion maker. Marco and Roco, who protected me when I first arrived at Stonehill and who now serve as part of my royal guard. Kara with her golden hair and Julian with her green eyes, the Fae girls who tended to my needs in Stonehill and later at Sky Castle, and who now own their own business. My mother, holding our baby. Seri, the healer. Es and Pete. Durk and Madrid. Kayla and Tavian. Asher and Varis. Zeb and Ace.

We reach the altar and face each other, holding hands.

Baron walks down next, carrying our rings on a pillow on his back, Yami and Riku sitting on his shoulders.

Dean officiates, dressed in official black robes. He threatened to come shirtless, but acquiesced when Fen threatened to punch him. Some things never change. He goes through all the necessary political mumbo-jumbo, and then gets personal, as we make our vows much like we did a year ago. There are cheers in the crowd. And tears.

Most of all Dean's. He speaks through heavy emotion. "And so I, as Fen's brother, and Arianna's dearest friend, and as the person responsible for the birth of their child...oh, bloody hell this is so hard." He pulls out a handkerchief, wiping away his tears. "I pronounce you husband and wife. King and Queen. You may kiss each other already you bloody bastards."

And so Fen wraps me in his arms and presses his lips against mine. And together, we become rulers of Inferna and Avakiri. The Midnight Star and the Moonlight Prince. Vampire and Fae. Together at last.

I turn to the cheering crowd, tears in my eyes. There is still much work to be done, but for the first time in a long time, I breathe easy.

Dum Spiro Spero.

While I breathe, I hope.

THE END

Call us Karpov Kinrade. We're the husband and wife team behind *Vampire Girl*. And we want to say...Thank you for reading it. We worked hard on these characters and this world, and we're thrilled to share this story with so many readers. We hope you enjoyed *Moonlight Prince*, the final book in this fantasy series. Thank you so much for joining us on this journey. We are sad to see it end. If you are interested in our other work, sign up for the Karpov Kinrade/Vampire Girl newsletter and get all that and more!

And visit KarpovKinrade.com for more great books to read. If you're looking for something new and exciting, check out *Court of Nightfall*. It's an epic adventure full of suspense, love, betrayal, friendship, and twists and turns that will leave you breathless.

ABOUT THE AUTHORS

Karpov Kinrade is the pen name for the husband and wife writing duo of USA TODAY bestselling, award-winning authors Lux Kinrade and Dmytry Karpov.

Together, they write fantasy and science fiction.

Look for more from Karpov Kinrade in *The Nightfall Chronicles* and *The Forbidden Trilogy*. If you're looking for their suspense and romance titles, you'll now find those under Alex Lux.

They live with three little girls who think they're ninja princesses with super powers and who are also showing a propensity for telling tall tales and using the written word to weave stories of wonder and magic.

Find them online at KarpovKinrade.com

On Facebook/KarpovKinrade

On Twitter @KarpovKinrade

And subscribe to their newsletter for special deals and up-to-date notice of new launches.

~~~~~

If you enjoyed this book, consider supporting the author by leaving a review wherever you purchased this book. Thank you.

Made in the USA
Lexington, KY
27 October 2017